# DYE HARD

MORGANA BEST

Dye Hard
Australian Amateur Sleuth, Book 3
Copyright © 2016 by Morgana Best
All rights reserved.
ISBN 9781925674255

No part of this book may be reproduced in any form or by any electronic or mechanical means, including information storage and retrieval systems, without written permission from the author, except for the use of brief quotations in a book review.

This is a work of fiction. Any resemblance to any person, living or dead, is purely coincidental. The personal names have been invented by the author, and any likeness to the name of any person, living or dead, is purely coincidental.

This book may contain references to specific commercial products, process or service by trade name, trademark, manufacturer, or otherwise, specific brand-name products and/or trade names of products, which are trademarks or registered trademarks and/or trade names, and these are property of their respective owners. Morgana Best or her associates, have no association with any specific commercial products, process, or service by trade name, trademark, manufacturer, or otherwise, specific brand-name products and / or trade names of products.

# GLOSSARY

Some Australian spellings and expressions are entirely different from US spellings and expressions. Below are just a few examples. It would take an entire book to list all the differences.

The author has used Australian spelling in this series. Here are a few examples: *Mum* instead of the US spelling *Mom*, *neighbour* instead of the US spelling *neighbor*, *realise* instead of the US spelling *realize*. It is *Ms*, *Mr* and *Mrs* in Australia, not *Ms.*, *Mr.* and *Mrs.*; *defence* not *defense; judgement* not *judgment; cosy* and not *cozy; 1930s* not *1930's*; *offence* not *offense*; *centre* not *center*; *towards* not *toward*; *jewellery* not *jewelry*; *favour* not *favor*; *mould* not *mold*; *two storey house* not *two story house*; *practise* (verb) not *practice* (verb); *odour* not *odor*; *smelt* not *smelled*; *travelling* not *traveling; liquorice* not *licorice; cheque* not *check; leant* not *leaned; have concussion* not *have a concussion; anti clockwise* not *counterclockwise; go to hospital* not *go to the hospital; sceptic* not *skeptic; aluminium* not *aluminum; learnt* not *learned*. We have *fancy dress* parties not *costume* parties. We don't say *gotten*. We say *car crash* (or *accident*) not *car wreck*. We say *a herb* not *an herb* as we produce the 'h.'

We might say (a company name) *are* instead of *is*.

The above are just a few examples.

It's not only different words; Aussies sometimes use different expressions in sentence structure. We might *eat a curry* not *eat curry*. We might say *in the main street* not *on the main street*. Someone might be *going well* instead of *doing well*. We might say *without drawing breath* not *without drawing a breath*.

These are just some of the differences.

Please note that these are not mistakes or typos, but correct, normal Aussie spelling, terms, and syntax.

## AUSTRALIAN SLANG AND TERMS

Benchtops - counter tops (kitchen)
Big Smoke - a city

Blighter - infuriating or good-for-nothing person
Blimey! - an expression of surprise
Bloke - a man (usually used in nice sense, "a good bloke")
Blue (noun) - an argument ("to have a blue")
Bluestone - copper sulphate (copper sulfate in US spelling)
Bluo - a blue laundry additive, an optical brightener
Boot (car) - trunk (car)
Bonnet (car) - hood (car)
Bore - a drilled water well
Budgie smugglers (variant: budgy smugglers) - named after the Aussie native bird, the budgerigar. A slang term for brief and tight-fitting men's swimwear
Bugger! - as an expression of surprise, not a swear word
Bugger - as in "the poor bugger" - refers to an unfortunate person (not a swear word)
Bunging it on - faking something, pretending
Bush telegraph - the grapevine, the way news spreads by word of mouth in the country
Car park - parking lot
Cark it - die
Chooks - chickens
Come good - turn out okay

Copper, cop - police officer
Coot - silly or annoying person
Cream bun - a sweet bread roll with copious amounts of cream, plus jam in the centre
Crook - 1. "Go crook (on someone)" - to berate them. 2. (someone is) crook - (someone is) ill. 3. Crook (noun) - a criminal
Demister (in car) - defroster
Drongo - an idiot
Dunny - an outhouse, an outdoor toilet building, often ramshackle
Fair crack of the whip - a request to be fair, reasonable, just
Flannelette (fabric) - cotton, wool, or synthetic fabric, one side of which has a soft finish.
Flat out like a lizard drinking water - very busy
Galah - an idiot
Garbage - trash
G'day - Hello
Give a lift (to someone) - give a ride (to someone)
Goosebumps - goose pimples
Gumboots - rubber boots, wellingtons
Knickers - women's underwear
Laundry (referring to the room) - laundry room
Lamingtons - iconic Aussie cakes, square, sponge, chocolate-dipped, and coated with desiccated

coconut. Some have a layer of cream and strawberry jam (= jelly in US) between the two halves.

Lift - elevator

Like a stunned mullet - very surprised

Mad as a cut snake - either insane or very angry

Mallee bull (as fit as, as mad as) - angry and/or fit, robust, super strong.

Miles - while Australians have kilometres these days, it is common to use expressions such as, "The road stretched for miles," "It was miles away."

Moleskins - woven heavy cotton fabric with suede-like finish, commonly used as working wear, or as town clothes

Mow (grass / lawn) - cut (grass / lawn)

Neenish tarts - Aussie tart. Pastry base. Filling is based on sweetened condensed milk mixture or mock cream. Some have layer of raspberry jam (jam = jelly in US). Topping is in two equal halves: icing (= frosting in US), usually chocolate on one side, and either lemon or pink or the other.

Pub - The pub at the south of a small town is often referred to as the 'bottom pub' and the pub at the north end of town, the 'top pub.' The size of a small town is often judged by the number of pubs - i.e. "It's a three pub town."

Red cattle dog - (variant: blue cattle dog usually known as a 'blue dog') - referring to the breed of Australian Cattle Dog. However, a 'red dog' is usually a red kelpie (another breed of dog)
Shoot through - leave
Shout (a drink) - to buy a drink for someone
Skull (a drink) - drink a whole drink without stopping
Stone the crows! - an expression of surprise
Takeaway (food) - Take Out (food)
Toilet - also refers to the room if it is separate from the bathroom
Torch - flashlight
Tuck in (to food) - to eat food hungrily
Ute /Utility - pickup truck
Vegemite - Australian food spread, thick, dark brown
Wardrobe - closet
Windscreen - windshield

## Indigenous References

Bush tucker - food that occurs in the Australian bush

*Koori* - the original inhabitants/traditional custodians of the land of Australia in the part of NSW in which this book is set. *Murri* are the people just to the north. White European culture often uses the term, *Aboriginal people*.

CHAPTER 1

"It's good to be able to relax, at long last," Mr Buttons said, leaning back in his chair comfortably. It was hard to disagree, though with a mouthful of tea I couldn't tell him so.

We had been sitting in the dining room for a few minutes. There were only the three of us. Firstly, there was Mr Buttons, the eccentric older English man with an unfortunate penchant for cleanliness. It doesn't seem like such a flaw, but I was almost certain he had a form of obsessive compulsive disorder. I'd seen him wipe food from a stranger's face and think nothing of it.

He wasn't without his redeeming features, of course. He made a mean cucumber sandwich—a lot better than it sounds—as well as having a knack for brewing the perfect tea, yet I was sure it was partly due to how expensive the tea itself always was. I almost felt bad for drinking it, though Mr Buttons always selflessly offered some.

Essentially, he was everything one would expect from a stereotypical butler, and I often (and only half-jokingly) wondered if he'd harboured Batman at some point in his life. Of course, he wasn't a butler at all, simply Cressida's only permanent boarder.

"Yesh," Cressida mumbled in agreement with a mouth full of cucumber sandwich. "Excuse me. Yes, I agree." Cressida was, as always, wearing an unbearable amount of makeup. Her long, bright—and I do mean *bright*—red hair flowed over her face, and I couldn't help but think she looked a little like a clown. It was as if somebody had told her to "make up her mind" and she'd taken their advice too literally.

I don't mean to be rude, though. Cressida was a good friend, and she'd always been there to help me when I needed it.

"I've even had time to paint a new piece," Cressida declared, interrupting my thoughts. She held up a large canvas to show us her new work, possibly in an attempt to stop us from sleeping comfortably ever again. Mr Buttons nearly choked on his tea, and for the briefest of moments I nearly passed out. It would have been a mercy.

I'd forgotten to mention—and had tried to forget completely—but Cressida had a bizarre habit of painting incredibly gory scenes. This time, she'd opted to paint a scene of a shipwreck, in which at least thirty sailors were being killed in increasingly awful ways. At least, I think it was about thirty sailors. It was hard to tell when their limbs were scattered all over the canvas.

"That's uh..." I struggled to think of something that wasn't a lie, but also wouldn't hurt Cressida's feelings. "Well, it sure is something. It's so unique, and you've made it so vibrant. I love all the blues and dull tones contrasted against the, uh, different shades of the red blood."

"Thank you, Sibyl!" Cressida beamed, putting the canvas away. Mr Buttons and I simultaneously sighed in relief. "I can't hang it anywhere in the boarding house because it reminds people of the murders," Cressida said, sadly. I refrained from suggesting that it probably shouldn't be put anywhere but a furnace.

There had been a murder not too long ago. The gardener had poisoned some academics who were boarding. It was awful, and I wanted nothing more than to forget it completely.

"I'm not quite sure it fits the décor, if I'm honest, Cressida," Mr Buttons suggested helpfully, although I disagreed. The boarding house was a large and grand Victorian mansion, every bit as cliché as one could imagine. I could scarcely believe it existed the first time I'd seen it.

Cressida had been using it as a boarding house, which is how we'd met. I still hadn't become used to the dusty old antiques, though, and I thought that Cressida's terrifying paintings would add a not-at-all needed haunted feel, if only to complete the stereotype.

"Perhaps, yes." Cressida sighed again and sat the painting aside. "Either way, I suppose it isn't going up anywhere."

"Perhaps you could sell them?" I suggested in an attempt to get the paintings further away from me. I realised that anybody who'd want to buy something like this was somebody I wouldn't really want to meet, but pushed that thought to the back of my mind.

"Oh, come now, Sibyl." Cressida laughed. "They're not good enough to sell." For the first time I found myself agreeing with Cressida about the quality of her paintings, although it was the subject matter that I had a problem with. I decided not to argue with her, knowing that I could neither convince her otherwise nor handle thinking about the paintings for much longer.

I took another bite of my cucumber sandwich —crusts removed, as Mr Buttons always ensured— and swallowed it with some more expensive tea. It sounded a strange combination, and I supposed it was, but I'd become used to it at this point.

I'd thoroughly enjoyed my time since I'd moved here, horrible murders aside. I figured that so many murders in a row made it statistically impossible that more would occur, or even just incredibly unlikely. I didn't think I had much to worry about.

I often found myself simply enjoying the atmosphere. As the boarding house was in the Australian countryside, I'd often hear cows mooing from the neighbouring fields, and wake up to the sound of magpies singing. Typical Australian countryside, perhaps, but it was certainly preferable to the sirens and drunken slurs of the inner-city. Although I could do without the Tawny Frogmouth Owls and their horrendous screeching, they were uncommon enough that it didn't bother me too often.

In all, it was an incredibly peaceful and overall enjoyable place to live. That was before the murders, of course. It had been very hard to settle back into daily life once you'd been so close to such a severe crime, but it was beginning to fall into place again. I was looking forward to returning to a life of normalcy.

"Yes, they're coming to hunt ghosts," Cressida said with a smile. I'd been too lost in thought to pay attention, but Cressida and Mr Buttons had been talking without me. I realised I needed to catch up, though I wasn't sure I wanted to.

"Who's coming to hunt what?" I asked, immediately realising I didn't want to know the answer. Surely I'd misheard her.

"Ghosts, dear. Some professionals are coming to hunt ghosts in town." Cressida explained it like I was an idiot for not understanding immediately, and took a long sip of tea. I really had no idea how to react, and looked to Mr Buttons for guidance.

He, too, was drinking tea, seemingly unperturbed at the idea of ghost hunters coming to stay in the boarding house. "How long do you think they'll be staying, Cressida?" he asked flatly.

"Oh, I can't say for certain. Until their work is done, I suppose," Cressida explained thoughtfully.

"I must admit to having some reservations at the idea," Mr Buttons said, and I sighed with relief as he did. I thought I'd been going mad for thinking it was all a bit strange. "They perhaps might cause an awful mess," Mr Buttons continued.

My jaw dropped open. "Hang on a second." I took a deep breath and continued. "Do neither of you think it at least a little bit strange that ghost hunters are coming to stay? How can you both be so nonchalant about the whole thing?" I was exasperated.

"Well, I suspect they're here because of the murders." Cressida nodded.

I sighed, and spoke again. "Cressida, I realise that, but do you think it's a good idea? Whether or not you believe in this kind of thing isn't even my problem. What if they either find something or pretend they do? That can't be good for business." As I said it, I realised that maybe I was wrong. Business wasn't exactly booming at the boarding house, but maybe a haunted house would bring more customers in. Cressida's paintings would certainly fit the new décor.

"Oh, that's a good point, dear," Cressida said thoughtfully. "Still, I'm sure the place isn't haunted. Probably. Hopefully. But they'll put my mind at ease either way." She smiled before taking another drink of her tea.

"Do you know exactly what they'll be doing here?" Mr Buttons asked her. He was always the sensible one. Even though I was sure that he was simply worried about the mess that they could cause, I had to admit to being curious about it as well. There was something about the idea that really didn't sit well with me. Possibly the ghost hunting part.

"Not exactly, no," Cressida admitted. "Hunting ghosts, I suppose."

Mr Buttons sighed. "How exactly does one go about doing so?"

Cressida seemed at a loss, but I thought maybe I could help. "I think they use electromagnetic wave readers, for one thing. I couldn't tell you how they work, but they sense some kind of special energy that ghosts and spirits supposedly emit." As I spoke, I noticed Cressida and Mr Buttons looking at me with their eyebrows raised. Undeterred, I pushed on. "They also call out and ask spirits to make a noise or answer in return, and record it all with night vision cameras. Haven't you ever seen *Most Haunted*?"

"Night vision cameras?" Cressida asked. "Why

on earth would they need those? It's well lit in here." It was hard to disagree when there was so much light reflecting from her over-applied bronzer, but I deigned to explain it anyway.

"Well, they do most of their ghost hunting in the dark, at night. They set up cameras in certain areas, but they also walk around and try to capture some footage with small teams." I shrugged.

"Why would they do that?" Cressida asked. "Do ghosts even care about night and day?"

I realised that it was a reasonable question. "I suppose it's just to make the footage more atmospheric," I suggested, not really knowing for certain.

"And how do you know all of this, Sibyl? A left-behind career of which we're not aware?" Mr Buttons asked, clearly taking an interest.

I laughed, and for a brief moment thought it would be fun to just let them keep thinking I'd been a ghost hunter. "No, nothing that exciting, unfortunately," I explained. "I've just seen a lot of those kinds of shows. They're quite popular. Like I said, I watched *Most Haunted* for years."

"It's a bunch of silly nonsense!" a voice declared from behind me, causing all present to nearly jump out of their seats. It was Dorothy, the new cook, storming in and spewing forth her opinion, as was the norm. "Ghosts and spirits aren't real, and these people are just going to ruin the business."

Mr Buttons looked less than impressed with this display, but remained quiet. I didn't really know what to say in defence of Cressida, and felt a tinge of shame that I didn't speak up. Luckily, she was more than capable of defending herself.

"Dorothy, the only threat to the business is a cook who spends more time complaining and stomping about than she does cooking. We have guests in need of sustenance, so please get back to work."

Mr Buttons and I dropped our jaws in shock, and Dorothy was gone before I even had a chance to see her reaction.

Cressida was no stranger to bad staff—most employers never had to deal with murderers as she had—but it was rare that she was so firm with somebody. Not that I wasn't impressed, but knowing she had such a strong side certainly made her paintings all the more unsettling.

CHAPTER 2

There were five of them in total. I watched as they got out of their black SUV and walked towards the estate. As I stood alongside Mr Buttons and Cressida, I wondered if these strangers would actually find a ghost.

The one at the front had black hair and an infectious smile, but there was something undeniably slimy about him. Behind him was a taller man, who was bald with a beard. His arms were covered in tattoos. He looked like a biker, only even more intimidating.

The third was a woman, about my height. She had striking red hair and was dressed more casually than the others. Walking behind her was a man wearing a brightly coloured scarf and a black hat.

Finally, there was a shorter man with a goatee. He walked with a skip in his step, and I felt he was the only one in the group that seemed outwardly friendly. *Then again*, I said to myself, *do friendly people hunt ghosts for a living? What sort of person does?*

Dorothy snorted. As I said, she was the new cook here at the boarding house. Since Alison the maid had been thrown in jail, Cressida was having a hard time keeping up with all the orders. As such, a new cook had been hired—Dorothy. And Dorothy was awful.

Dorothy was a middle-aged woman, although her hair was already completely white, and tied back in a severe knot. She had made it abundantly clear that she did not believe in the paranormal, nor did she approve of ghost hunters coming to investigate, though she had used the term *snoop around* in lieu of *investigate*.

Mr Buttons shot an angry sideways glance at Dorothy. As she had made it clear that she didn't believe in the paranormal, Mr Buttons had made it clear he didn't believe in Dorothy. He seemed to despise everything about her, although he hid it behind a passive-aggressive tone. He would say things like, "Ma'am, please refrain from carrying on in such a capacity," and that was as rude as he ever got. To be honest, while it was a little funny, I felt bad about how frustrated she made him. To top it all off, she couldn't cook as well as Cressida, so I had two reasons to dislike her.

When the ghost hunters made it to the front door, Cressida greeted the man at the front with a handshake and a smile. As they exchanged greetings and names, I caught myself day dreaming about the last few months. There had been three murders since I had arrived in the town of Little Tatterford. There weren't really such things as ghosts, were there?

"Hello." The man with the black hair reached his hand out to shake mine.

"Oh," I said. "Hello. Nice to meet you. I'm Sibyl." I took his hand and shook it. He smiled back at me and continued onto Dorothy without telling me his name. I didn't have time to think much of it, as the others came by and introduced themselves.

In the end, I found out all their names, even the first man, who turned out to be the leader of the group. His name was James. The bald man was Alex; the red haired woman was Sue; the man with the scarf was Michael, and finally, the man with the goatee was Ken. They all seemed quite friendly, though I felt there was something off about them. I couldn't quite figure it out, though it was probably just because they hunted ghosts for a living.

We were still milling about the entrance talking to one another. The weather was mild and the sky was overcast, though it didn't look as if rain was due any time soon. I got talking to Sue.

"So," I began, "you hunt ghosts? How?"

She smiled at this question, and I realised it was probably one of the first things anyone asked her. "Well, we have specialised equipment. We have electric thermometers, electromagnetic field readers, thermographic and night vision cameras, geophones and more. Obviously, we film it all, too." As she said this, she motioned to several large black bags, presumably full of equipment, sitting behind her.

"That sounds, well, expensive," I said. I couldn't understand how they could make a profit, so I asked her how they did it.

"Well, it isn't easy," she replied. "Some places pay quite a lot for footage, and some of us work other jobs. Some of us have worked as pharmacists, plumbers, lawyers—you name it. We work to make ends meet, and this is sometimes more of a passion project, though we're coming along nicely…"

Before she could finish, James stepped up to us

and interrupted her. "We're the best at what we do, plain and simple. Other ghost hunting teams come up with either circumstantial evidence, or simply nothing. We get results." At this, James and Sue shared a glance.

There definitely seemed to be some tension between them. Were they former—or current—lovers? I didn't really care. I'd had more than enough drama in my life, and romantic tension between expert ghost hunters wasn't something that drew my interest.

"You mentioned other teams?" I asked, keen to change the subject.

"Yes," James replied, smiling that infectious smile I'd seen earlier. "There aren't many, of course. It's not an easy field to make a living in, as you can imagine. I'd say we're one of three, maybe four teams in the whole country that even have the equipment to do it properly." As James spoke, I detected a definite tone of condescension, as if he were trying to explain a simple concept to a child.

"What sort of things have you found?" I asked the question quite earnestly, despite taking offence at his tone. While he might not be the easiest person to get along with—or so I assumed, from our brief encounter—he did follow an interesting career path.

"Oh, lots of things, all of which have been recorded on either film or tape. I assumed you would have taken the time to look us up, seeing that you knew we were coming."

I narrowed my eyes at James's arrogance. He had taken full control of this situation, and Sue was standing awkwardly to the side, as if she were trying to avoid the conversation altogether. I decided she had the right idea.

"Well, sorry, but I'd never even heard of you until this morning. It's not as if Cressida posted a big announcement, warning us all not to be blinded by the light of your glorious radiance when you finally saw fit to grace us with your presence." I was obviously being sarcastic, but James didn't take offence. Rather, he laughed out loud.

"I didn't mean to offend," he offered, still smiling. "It's just been a long trip, and as you can imagine, we have this same conversation every time we arrive somewhere new."

CHAPTER 3

It had been a few days since the ghost hunters had arrived. They'd settled in comfortably, although I found their presence more than a little unsettling. They weren't exactly quiet when they went about their investigations, and as they did so in the middle of the night, it made sleeping more than a little uncomfortable, even from the distance of my cottage. Knowing they were here specifically to look for ghosts didn't help, either.

They had been nice enough to me since their arrival, yet I still found them to be either generally obnoxious or just untrustworthy. I knew it was rude to think that about them, especially since these people hadn't actually done anything to me. At least, not on purpose. But the lack of sleep combined with their generally arrogant attitude was setting me on edge.

They weren't all so bad, though. James switched between being both charming and courteous to being obnoxious and rude. I suspected he was always the latter, but had practiced his façade. Still, he seemed harmless—at least, harmless compared to some of the people I'd met over the last few months or so.

Alex, the bald man, hadn't said a word to me, so it was hard to say how I felt about him. He seemed nice enough, but then he literally hadn't spoken since he got here. I wasn't sure if he was mute or just quiet. Either way, it was more than a little unsettling.

Michael was more than a little talkative, and insisted on wearing his scarf, despite the warm weather. I hadn't seen him without it even once. Was he hiding something, or did he just have poor fashion sense? He did seem to be genuinely nice, which was more than I could say for most of them. He had apologised more than once for the noise they'd been making, although he hadn't taken any efforts to stop it. I suspected that was due to his lack of power in the group, as James clearly had the final say in all matters.

Then there was Ken, the man with the goatee. He had been generally reclusive too, much like Alex, though Ken at least had spoken on occasion. He was friendly enough when he had, but on occasion would remain quiet even when asked a direct question. I found that quite unsettling.

Finally, there was Sue. She had been friendly to me on the day they arrived, but that was the last time we'd spoken. I'd heard her arguing a few times, though I couldn't tell with whom she was talking. Whoever it was, they were clearly not as loud as she was. I figured she was probably going through a break-up with James, though I still really had no idea if they were even a couple.

I was up earlier than usual, having walked my yellow labrador, Sandy, an hour earlier than usual due to predicted thunderstorms. I was sitting in my living room, enjoying a simple breakfast of peanut butter on toast, and coffee, when I heard a knock at my door. When I opened it, I saw Cressida standing there, hands on hips, and a furious look plastered on her face. "Oh, dear. What's wrong?" I asked.

"It's that woman!" Cressida yelled. I'd never seen her so angry. I was afraid she'd burst a blood vessel. "Come in and sit down," I offered. "I'll make you some tea." She graciously accepted and took a seat on my sofa. "Now, tell me what happened."

"It's *Dorothy*." Cressida practically spat the name. "She won't stop talking. I'm terribly sorry to speak so rudely of someone, but I can't stand it. How Mr Buttons handles her is beyond me."

I stepped back into the room with a fresh cup of tea and handed it to Cressida. "What has she done?" I asked. Normally I wouldn't be interested in these things, but I wanted something to distract me from the ghost hunters. There had been so much drama in my life since I'd moved here, so listening to someone complain about a co-worker sounded wonderfully normal.

"We were talking about that strange man, Alec, or whatever his name is…"

"Alex."

"Thank you, yes, Alex. Anyway, we were wondering why he never spoke, which is when Dorothy said…" Before Cressida could finish, there was a loud banging on the door. I jumped up immediately, startled, and ran to the door.

When I got there, it swung open. Standing in the doorway was Mr Buttons, looking flushed and sweating profusely. *Oh, great*, I thought. *Dorothy's done something to upset him as well*. Unfortunately, the truth was much worse.

Before I could ask what had happened, Mr Buttons told me. "Sue is dead!"

My first thought, strangely, was that at least he was to the point, and my second thought was that I might be becoming desensitised. My third thought —disbelief—was a lot more normal. "What do you mean, dead?" I asked. Of course, I knew exactly what he meant, but the question had to be asked. It's not as if murder is ever any easier. Assuming, of course, that it was indeed murder.

"I don't know what's happened. The ambulance is there right now, and the police have been called. I think she was *murdered*, Sibyl." Mr Buttons' voice was panic-stricken.

This was insane. One murder in your home is more than anybody should have to go through. Two is unbelievable. But four? I was starting to think that maybe the place really was haunted.

"How do you know she was murdered?" I asked.

Mr Buttons averted his gaze. "Well," he replied, "I don't know, really. But of course it was. Of all people, you would know. After I called the police, I came straight here. As if we ever have accidents here." He took a seat in the living room opposite Cressida.

I closed the front door behind him. Cressida's mouth was hanging open in shock, and her hand had been raised to cover it. She sat there, silently, all colour drained from her face.

I made a fresh batch of tea as we all sat in silence, before I finally spoke. "Exactly what happened?"

"I was just on my way to the kitchen and was walking past the bathroom on the east wing when I heard a loud thump," he said. "I knocked on the door and called out, but nobody answered. When I tried the handle, I found it unlocked, and saw her lying on the floor. It was strange, though."

*You found a dead body, and said something about it was strange,* I thought. *Aside from detectives and coroners, we're the only people on earth that wouldn't find the body itself to be strange.* I didn't say anything, and he continued.

"Well, there wasn't any blood. At least, not on the floor. But I think there was some in her hair."

"What could possibly cause that?" I asked. Mr Buttons simply shrugged at me and looked at the floor. Another day, another murder. Yet was she murdered, or had she simply slipped?

I sighed some more. Of course she hadn't

slipped. At that point, I fell straight into a vision. Cressida appeared before me. Her hair was a brighter red than usual, and she was running around my room, screaming. Suddenly, a different vision of Cressida appeared, with her hair the colour it is now. She was smiling, and sipping from a tea cup. The vision stopped as abruptly as it had begun.

CHAPTER 4

I sat with Cressida and Mr Buttons in the kitchen of the boarding house, waiting for the police and medical examiner to arrive.

I was unable to get rid of the sense of uneasiness, and chewed one thumbnail, occasionally exchanging glances with Cressida.

Mr Buttons was the first to speak. "It just doesn't make any sense. We didn't hear any screams. She didn't come out of the bathroom for help—although I think she tried as she was at the door, and it was unlocked—and nobody else was in there with her. What could have possibly happened to her?"

I shrugged my shoulders, while Cressida continued sipping her coffee. "It could have been anything, really," I said. "It's probably best to wait for the cops to sort it all out. We can guess all we'd like, but until some professionals who know what they're doing take a look, we're still stuck assuming."

"I guess you're right," Mr Buttons agreed. "Those ghost busters upstairs are going to be in for a shocker when they wake up either way, though."

"I wonder if the place really is haunted," I said aloud, but to myself.

"This place hasn't been haunted until today," Cressida protested. "And what's taking them so long?"

We sat in silence until the sound of a police siren made us all jump. We hurried to the front door.

Blake walked up to the door with a thin, older man walking beside him.

He simply shook his head, his expression grim. "This way," Mr Buttons said.

Mr Buttons led the solemn procession, Blake and the man behind him, and Cressida bringing up the rear.

Blake turned to Cressida. "Was deceased one of the ghost investigation team?"

Cressida nodded. "Her name is Sue, and she

came here with four other team members, all men. It was completely unexpected."

"It usually is," Blake said. "So, there were no signs that could have led any of you to believe something was going to happen to her?"

I shook my head. "Do you think something was done to her?" I did not want to use the term *murdered*.

Blake glanced around the narrow corridor. "It's impossible to tell until we get in there and see what the scene tells us." He motioned for the doctor to follow him into the bathroom, and then turned to Mr Buttons. "Please stay out here and make sure nobody disturbs us while we investigate."

Mr Buttons nodded. "Of course."

Blake closed the door as he disappeared into the bathroom. Mr Buttons motioned to us to join him, and we all leant close with our ears to the door.

There was no sound for a few moments, and then Blake spoke. "What do you think, Doctor Smythe?"

"I'm thinking this looks like a case of anaphylaxis. I'd say the manner of death was natural."

Cressida, Mr Buttons, and I exchanged glances. "You think?"

I could tell Blake's voice held more than a note of disbelief.

"All signs point to it. See these red patches on her forearm, here? Those are hives from an allergic reaction. And look here. See the swelling around the throat and mouth? She must have gone into shock using this hair dye. It's a well-known brand, so that is just another reason to rule out any sort of tampering."

Again, here was silence for a few moments, and the three of us leant even closer to the door.

"Can you at least run a tox screen on the victim?"

"She's not a *victim*, Sergeant," the man said sternly. "I don't think it's necessary, to be entirely honest."

Blake pressed on. "So, is anaphylaxis common?"

"I wouldn't say it's common, *per se*. It does happen, however, and not infrequently."

"I think I'll at least have the forensics team collect that bottle for testing. If something foreign was added to the lotion, it could have triggered the reaction."

"Sergeant, I truly think you're over thinking this. It's clear-cut. The girl needed medical attention immediately and went into shock before she was able to find help. It was a natural death, I assure you."

Blake grunted and let out a loud sigh. Seconds later, the door swung open, and the three of us jumped back, doing our best to appear as if we hadn't been listening into the conversation.

Blake narrowed his eyes at us. "Well, it seems as if the doctor has determined the death was from natural causes. I don't need to tell you not to go in there, and an ambulance will be along soon to collect the body. I'll be right back." With that, he hurried down the corridor with the doctor.

"What do we do?" Cressida said. "This is the only bathroom on the east wing. The ghost hunters will be awake soon, and they'll want to use the bathroom. Should I put an *Out Of Order* sign on the door and lock it?"

I had no idea what to do, so I was relieved when Mr Buttons spoke. "Blake shouldn't be too long. Let's just wait here, and Blake can break the news to them."

Several minutes later, Blake walked back inside without the older man. "Sorry for walking out like that, but I just don't agree with his assessment of the scene. Something just seems out of place, but it's more of a gut feeling than anything else."

I frowned. "What do you mean?"

"Allergic reactions usually give someone time to react, even if it's only enough time to call for help. People who have known severe allergic reactions carry an adrenaline autoinjector with them, and they obviously have time to inject it. None of you heard her calling for anyone or screaming in pain, right?"

"I didn't hear anything except a loud bang," Mr Buttons said. "Not a peep otherwise. Anyway, what about an autopsy? Is one being done?"

Blake was clearly frustrated. "Doctor Smythe isn't open to performing one on the victim. He's so sure her death was due to natural causes that he won't even take the time to look into it further."

I sighed. "Blake, if someone did this, who could it be, and what would be their reasoning behind it? It wouldn't make much sense."

Blake frowned. "Murder never makes sense. We're going to treat it like a natural passing, but if anything else happens that seems out of place, call me right away. Don't hesitate. Now I'll have to track down her next of kin. I'll need to speak to the other members of her team."

Right at that moment, I heard the creaking of the old, tallow wood floor boards as the four men from the ghost hunting team climbed down the stairs. I bit my lip. They were in for most unpleasant and distressing news. I wanted to be anywhere but here.

"What's going on?" James asked. "Why are the police here?" The others stood behind him, their jaws open in surprise.

Ken pushed forward to the front of the group. "Why are the cops here?"

Mr Buttons, Cressida, and I all looked at Blake.

James looked around frantically. "Wait a minute, where's Sue?" A look of panic washed over his face. "Has something happened to Sue?"

Blake stepped forward. "I'm Sergeant Blake Wessley. I'm sorry to have to tell you this, but Sue was found deceased this morning."

The four men gasped in unison and James's hand flew to his throat. "What happened? She was just fine last night!" His voice broke into a choke.

"We haven't ascertained the cause of death yet, but we will be looking into it."

Confused, I spoke. "But I thought…"

Blake's withering glare silenced me. He turned back to the ghost hunters. "Right now we think the hair dye she was using at the time of death played a role. It could have been natural, an allergic reaction, or it might have been from some tampering. We're going to run some tests and then we'll know for sure. There's no point in speculating until we do know for sure."

I didn't know anything about police procedure, but I wondered if Blake would be able to investigate despite the doctor saying the death was by natural causes. My best guess was that Blake did suspect foul play, and saw the ghost hunters as the most likely bunch of suspects.

James crossed his arms over his chest. "So, you're telling me one of my closest friends is gone and you can't even tell me why?" His tone was belligerent.

Blake's frown deepened. "As I already stated, we won't know for sure until we run tests."

James stepped back. "This is ridiculous. She was just fine last night."

Ken tapped his arm. "Hey man, maybe we should head back home and take a break from this stuff for a bit."

James turned to Ken. "What? Are you serious? We need this. For all we know, the ghosts could have done this to her. We aren't going anywhere!"

"You're right. You guys are staying put until we know for sure what happened here," Blake said. "Now, may I ask the whereabouts of each of you this morning?" He pulled a small notebook from his pocket and readied a pen. He glanced at the men, waiting for an answer.

"We were all here," Ken said, "sleeping."

"Yeah, asleep," James added. He then sank to the ground and sobbed wildly, his shoulders shaking.

Alex patted his shoulder awkwardly, while Mr Buttons, Cressida and I looked at each other, at a loss what to do.

Michael bent over James, muttering words of comfort, while Alex just stood there, his hands on his hips.

"What's going on here?" Dorothy's strident voice cut through the tense atmosphere.

"Dorothy, Sue has died," Cressida said.

Dorothy gasped. "What? Sue died?"

We all nodded.

"Can you tell me what you were doing this morning?" Blake asked her, but the question did not go over well.

"Slaving over a hot stove making cooked breakfasts, that's what!" she exclaimed rudely, waving a stubby fist at Blake. "And no one came down for breakfast, so all the food's wasted!" Her voice rose to a high pitch. I wondered if all the antique glassware would crack.

Mr Buttons' face turned a ghastly shade of red. "Madam, please desist and refrain from this unseemly manner of conduct. There is a deceased person present."

Michael, Alex, and Ken looked at each other with barely veiled excitement. I expect they thought that Mr Buttons meant that he had sensed a ghost.

Dorothy narrowed her eyes and glared at Mr Buttons. "This is what happens when people start to mess with the occult! First your tarot cards," —she nearly spat the words— "and now these ghost busters. No good will come of it. You mark my words!" She waved her fist at all of us and then disappeared back down the corridor.

Blake walked closer to Mr Buttons. "Keep an eye on these guys," he said in a whispered tone. "Please call me if any of them try taking off or make any suspicious comments, or anything, anything at all."

Mr Buttons nodded, and I watched the ghost hunters as they stood there, trying in vain to comfort James.

CHAPTER 5

*I* walked into the boarding house and headed for the kitchen. On my way, I came across Cressida sitting next to the landline, her head down, and sipping from a coffee mug. "Good morning," I said.

Cressida let out a scream. "Whoa! You scared me. Lord Farringdon didn't tell me you were coming."

I sat on the over-stuffed, plush red velvet, antique grandmother chair next to her and looked down at the fat, tabby and white cat sitting at Cressida's feet. "Naughty Lord Farringdon."

He glared at me, his cheeks puffed out. I thought of my vision. "Cressida, perhaps it's a good idea if you don't dye your hair for a while, given what happened to Sue."

"Sure. I'm waiting on a call from the plumber," Cressida said. "He said he'll call when he's free and I need him to hurry back right now. He said he'd have my private bathroom finished by today, but he had the nerve to get called out on an emergency. What could be more of an emergency than me having to use the east wing bathroom while mine is out of action? That's where Sue was, well, you know."

I nodded in sympathy.

"Anyway," Cressida continued, "Lord Farringdon told me that not having my bathroom fixed by now will actually cause an emergency."

I raised my eyebrows but said nothing. "It would be easy if you had a mobile phone," I said. "Then you wouldn't have to sit around by this ancient landline." I pointed to the old-fashioned, black handset on the wall. "It's not even cordless," I added.

Cressida pulled back the folds of her outsized, golden and sky blue sarong to reveal an old-fashioned pager on her belt. "This little guy warns me whenever the phone rings. It's brilliant."

I fought the urge to laugh. "Sounds like a plan."

At the sound of a door banging, Cressida leaped to her feet. "Finally! Someone has been in that bathroom for a good twenty minutes." She stormed off to claim her turn.

I smiled and walked down to the kitchen to get myself a coffee. No one else was in the kitchen, so I sipped my coffee, my mind on recent events. I thought back to earlier days, and how everything now seemed so much more complicated in comparison. Was this a natural event or a brutal one?

The sound of the landline ringing made me jump, so lost was I in thought. I hurried to the front desk, concerned that Cressida's ancient pager might not work. I reached the landline, and stretched out my hand for the old receiver, when I saw Cressida hurrying towards me. My first thought was that her hair was covered in bright red dye. My second thought was that Cressida was staggering. My third thought was that Cressida had not heeded my warning about not dyeing her hair.

Cressida hit the floor just as Mr Buttons arrived on the scene. Without hesitation, I reached for the phone, which had now stopped ringing, and called the Australian Emergency number, 000. I gave them the address and then hung up, then called the police station.

"Sibyl," Mr Buttons called frantically, "quick, wash it out of her hair! The poison must be in the dye!"

I ran to Cressida who was shaking on the floor. "We can't drag her," Mr Buttons said, "Quick, fetch water!"

I ran down to the east wing bathroom and mercifully found a plastic pitcher. I filled it with water and grabbed some towels and ran back to Cressida.

Mr Buttons and I put towels under her head, and I poured the water over her head, at once drying it with towels.

"It must be readily absorbed by the skin," Mr Buttons said. "Wash it off your hands each time you go for water."

And so I ran between the bathroom and Cressida, pouring water on her head and drying off the excess, and I repeated the process, until at last sirens wailed.

Blake burst into the corridor, followed by two paramedics.

Mr Buttons stood up. "Blake, it's the red hair

dye, just the same as Sue. She was dyeing her hair…"

I interrupted him. "And she ran out to answer the phone, so the hair dye couldn't have been in for long and we washed it out, as best we could."

The paramedics already had Cressida on a stretcher with an oxygen mask on her face. It seemed to my relief that she was breathing more easily. They took her outside with Blake and me following hard on their heels. "We had a death here yesterday from hair dye," Blake told them. "It must be a toxin absorbed by the skin."

As they took Cressida away, sirens blaring, I looked around for Mr Buttons. He appeared at the door, just as Blake hurried back into the building.

I stood there, in shock, clutching Mr Buttons' arm. Neither of us spoke until Blake reappeared, holding a plastic bag containing a bottle. "This is another bottle of hair dye," he said. "The bathroom is now a crime scene, and Constable Andrews is on his way. Whatever, you do, don't go in there. I've taken this bottle for testing. You said the ghost hunters are out for the day?"

We both nodded.

"Good, but Mr Buttons, can you give me their mobile phone numbers? I'll need to call them to tell them to avoid that bathroom. They might not take notice of the yellow tape."

I sat on the front steps, in a daze, while both Mr Buttons and Blake disappeared back inside the building. I only nodded to Constable Andrews when he arrived. Soon, Blake and Mr Buttons were back. Blake patted me on the shoulder, before driving away. Mr Buttons took my arm. "Come on, Sibyl. Let's go to the hospital and see how Cressida is."

I followed Mr Buttons to his car, an old, green Bentley that looked as though it had been manufactured in the 1980's. Despite the car's elderly yet pristine appearance, the engine was powerful. Gravel flew everywhere as it surged down the driveway.

In no time at all, we arrived at the emergency room wing of the hospital, where we managed to find a parking spot fairly easily, and we made our way inside. My heart was in my mouth, wondering how Cressida was.

The nurse behind the desk looked up.

"Hi," I said. "Our friend, Cressida Upthorpe, was just rushed in here by ambulance. We wanted to know her condition."

The woman frowned. "Are you her relatives?"

"No, but…" I said, but Mr Buttons cut me off.

"Yes, I'm her husband, and this is her daughter-in-law."

My mouth fell open, until I remembered that hospitals often refused to give out any information to non relatives.

The woman frowned. "I'll just check for you." She walked through a side door. When she didn't return after a minute or so, Mr Buttons and I took a seat.

The nurse returned through her door just as the emergency room door opened, and a young, handsome doctor stepped out. He looked at us. "Are you two here to see Cressida Upthorpe?"

We nodded.

He motioned for us to follow. He led us into a small room and closed the door.

I feared the worst, and so apparently did Mr Buttons, given the way he was clutching my arm, his long, bony fingers digging in painfully.

"Ms Upthorpe is in a stable condition. She got lucky," the doctor said.

I breathed a long sigh of relief, while Mr Buttons said, "Got lucky?"

The doctor nodded. "Something interrupted her. Whatever caused this was in the hair dye. Given that the police have informed me of the recent death due to what they say is the same hair dye, it is something readily absorbed by the skin."

"She stopped dyeing her hair to answer the phone," I said, "and we washed it out as best we could."

"Will she be all right?" Mr Buttons' voice was strained.

The young doctor looked reluctant to speak, but answered regardless. "We can't make any promises, of course, but at this stage, it looks as if she will make a complete recovery."

Both Mr Buttons and I let out a long sigh in unison. I was so thankful that I thought I would burst into tears from sheer relief.

"Can we see her now?" Mr Buttons asked.

"If you can wait twenty minutes or so," the doctor said, "she will have a room." He nodded, and left the room, leaving us sitting there.

"Thank goodness she's okay," I said.

Mr Buttons nodded, and wiped a tear from one eye with an embroidered, linen handkerchief. "She gave me quite a fright."

"Who would want to kill Cressida?"

Mr Buttons shrugged. "Cressida and Sue had nothing in common. It might be the case that Sue was the target, and some hair dye meant for Sue was left in the bathroom."

"You would think the murderer would clear away the evidence, though."

Mr Buttons scratched his head. "It's beyond me. The main thing is that Cressida's okay."

I agreed. "Where will we wait?"

"The hospital cafeteria," Mr Buttons said. "We have another twenty minutes, so we might as well wait somewhere away from the smell of disinfectant."

I wrinkled up my nose. I had never liked the smell of hospitals. Soon the two of us were sitting opposite each other at a small white plastic table on two uncomfortable red plastic chairs. We were sipping horrible-tasting coffee. "At least it's caffeine," I said aloud, to no one in particular.

Mr Buttons did not respond, but kept looking at his watch.

Finally, twenty minutes had passed. "It's been twenty minutes. Let's go and find Cressida's room." Mr Buttons stood up.

When we arrived at the front desk of the ward, the woman sitting behind the computer looked up with a smile on her face. "Hello, may I help you?"

"Yes," I said. "Our friend, Cressida Upthorpe,

was just given a room and the doctor told us we could go up and see her."

"Name?"

"Cressida Upthorpe," I repeated, more slowly this time.

The older woman slid on a large pair of glasses and pressed them to her nose. She clicked away on the computer's mouse while peering at the screen. "Room 308." She pointed down the hall. "Go down there. Take the first elevator on your right up to the second floor. Walk past the nurses' station and look for her room number on your right-hand side."

We thanked her, and hurried off. After the elevator ride up one floor, we stepped out and walked in the direction of Cressida's room. 306, 307, 308. There it was. I knocked on the door, but Mr Buttons walked straight in.

To my delight, Cressida was propped in bed, looking far better than my expectations. Blake stood beside her, with a notebook in his hands.

"Hey, you two," he said.

"It hurt so badly," Cressida said quietly.

"What did?" I asked, crossing the room to stand beside her bed.

"The hair dye. I'd only just started to put it on, when my pager went off." She took a deep breath before continuing. "It was hard to breathe, and I felt sick and dizzy. That's pretty much the last thing I remember, before waking up here."

Blake crossed his arms. "I've called in the detectives. This is going to be treated as an attempted murder, and Sue's death is going to be investigated as a murder." Blake nodded to us and then left the room.

LATER THAT AFTERNOON, I bathed two Persian show cats for the one client, and then I returned to my house. I fed Sandy and Max, and then threw a frozen dinner in the microwave. While it was being nuked, I took a quick shower. I was on edge; I could not get the day's events out of my mind.

I was about to get dressed when I heard a knock on the door. I threw on a silk bathrobe, which was the closest thing I could find. My sister, Phyto, had sent it back from China for me: it was a pretty, pale green, with embroidered dragons on it.

I opened the door to see Blake standing there. "Hi Sibyl, may I come in?"

"Of course." I stood back to let him in. Unfortunately, I forgot that Max was still in the living room. He bobbed his head up and down, and then squawked at me, "I love your outfit. Did it come with a pole?"

I opened the back door and Max flew outside. I rolled my eyes, wrapped my bath robe around me more tightly, and turned to Blake. "Would you like a cup of coffee, or something?"

Blake shook his head. "Thank you, but no."

I was disappointed, but he pressed on. "I have to rush away. They've brought a court appearance forward so I have to drive to Sydney tonight. I'll be away for few days, and I was wondering if you would mind Tiny for me."

"Yes, of course." Tiny was Blake's chihuahua. My labrador, Sandy, and Tiny were friends. They often played together at the dog park, and after the weekly dog training classes. I was secretly pleased that Blake had asked me to mind his dog. This surely meant that he did not have a girlfriend hiding somewhere. If he had a girlfriend, surely she would be the one to mind his dog. I smiled at my logic.

"Thanks, Sibyl." Blake beamed at me. "I do have some bad news, though."

"What? Not Cressida?"

Blake shook his head. "No, no. It's the detectives. They refuse to come to town to investigate. They say Sue's death was simply anaphylactic shock."

I was gobsmacked. "Well, what's going to happen?" I said.

Blake took a step closer to me. "Sibyl, I want you to be very careful. Call me if anything happens. Leave a message if I'm in court. I don't like going away at a time like this, but I have no choice. When I get back, I'll sort out the investigation."

CHAPTER 6

In the time that I had been living on the grounds of the boarding house, I had never been in Mr Buttons' room. I sat in it now, perched in a corner upon a wooden chair with a pale blue cushion affixed to the seat by two small strings wrapping around the back frame. Mr Buttons stood at his closet, pulling on a tan jacket over his usual button-up shirt. We were going to go down to my cottage, to have some privacy while we talked about the murder and Cressida's subsequent poisoning. I had been surprised when Mr Buttons had asked me up to his room while he finished getting ready, but it turned out that he had something to tell me that he simply couldn't wait to discuss.

Once his jacket was on, he turned and walked over to me. "I can't hold it in any longer, my dear." He clapped his hands together and smiled.

"What is it?" I asked.

"I managed to take some of the poison in Cressida's bottle of hair dye!"

My mouth fell open. "You what?"

"I took some of it, with all of the craziness going around, it wasn't very hard. I put it in a small vial. Anyway, that's not the important part."

"That's not the important part?" I asked. "I'd love to know what is."

"I sent it in for testing." A grin so massive spread across Mr Buttons' face that I could count every one of his white teeth.

"You sent it in for testing? Where? Who?"

"Let's get down to your place," he said, waving his hand at me. "The walls have ears, and all of that."

"But," I started, but he was already half out the door. I had no choice but to follow.

We went down the staircase together and out the front door. I waited until the path towards my house curved to the left, and the boarding house was lost behind a row of delightfully scented, lemon eucalyptus trees after which were a variety of wattle trees, before I turned to Mr Buttons.

"So what now?" I asked. It annoyed me a little to see that Mr Buttons was just as pleased with himself as he had been in his room.

"I sent it to be tested."

I was a little frustrated. "Yes, I realise that, but who exactly did you send it to?"

Mr Buttons threw up his hands. "Oh I don't know, some company I found on the internet. You send them something and pay a fee, and they tell you what it is."

I tried to process the information. "Okay, so you sent the poison to be tested. When do you get the results?"

"I paid a rush fee, so it should only be a few days."

We had reached my cottage, and Mr Buttons sat on the couch patting Sandy, while I went into my kitchen to make a pot of tea. After I put on the tea, I let Sandy into the back yard, while inadvertently letting in my foul-mouthed sulphur-crested cockatoo, Max.

"Hello, idiots," he squawked, landing on the sofa behind to Mr Buttons and pecking at his hair. "Oh look, it's Dumb and Dumber."

"Max!" I scolded.

"*^&$%#" was Max's reply, so I caught him and put him out the back door, too.

When I returned, I poured the tea, handed Mr Buttons his cup and saucer and then sat next to him on the couch. We both took a moment to take a sip of tea and then we looked at one another.

"You do realise that Blake will have the poisonous hair dye tested, don't you?"

Mr Buttons nodded. "Yes, but Blake is away in Sydney in court, and nothing's happening right now."

I agreed. "You do have a point." I was going to say more, when I heard a shout from outside.

Mr Buttons heard it as well. "What was that?"

I set my cup on the coffee table and stood up. We both walked to the front door. I pulled it open a crack. I saw nothing amiss, but then we heard the angry voice again, off to the left, towards the boarding house. Mr Buttons and I hurried outside, and skirted behind the row of wattle trees.

Mr Buttons caught my arm and I stopped in my tracks. From our vantage point behind the wattle trees, we could see Dorothy, the new cook, and her son, Frank. Dorothy's son, Frank, had visited her at the boarding house once or twice.

Dorothy had been the one yelling. I peered through the bushes, and saw she was wearing a white coat and bright orange plastic shoes as she stood on the side of the path with her son. They had come from the boarding house, no doubt, and I wondered if they were simply taking a walk, or whether they were coming to see me. I had no idea why they would come to see me, given that I hadn't said more than five words to either of them in the month since Dorothy had started the job.

"You idiot!" Dorothy screamed. She was holding a big, wooden spoon in her hand, and she pulled it back and then whacked her thirty year old son on the arm with it.

"Ouch," Frank yelled, rubbing his arm with his hand. "I'm sorry."

"I worked hard to get this job. And I'm too old to be working at all, much less hard, and here you are making it worse for me."

"I didn't know," Frank whimpered.

"Of course you didn't," Dorothy yelled. "You never do. How could you be so stupid as to tip off James about the boarding house! Why would you tell them there are ghosts here? There are no such things as ghosts! Do you think I wanted James here?"

"I didn't think."

"No, you never think!" Dorothy whacked Frank's arm again with the wooden spoon. With that, she threw up her arms and turned to face the direction of the boarding house. She hurried forward, leaving her adult son bounding after her.

Mr Buttons and I looked at one another. "What's that about?" I whispered. "She and Frank seem to know James."

Mr Buttons scratched his head. "Dorothy hasn't let on that she knows James, and James certainly didn't let on that he knew Dorothy. How strange."

"What's going on?"

Mr Buttons simply shrugged.

"I wish we could find out."

"I'll keep an ear open. Perhaps you should come to dinner this evening."

I nodded. "Thanks, I will."

Mr Buttons and I parted company, and I returned to my cottage. I had only been sitting in the cottage for a short time, listening to my cockatoo insult me for a few minutes, when I pulled my shoes back on and went outside.

I didn't know exactly where I was going, but I walked along the path towards the boarding house. When I reached the boarding house, I kept walking, and then made my way down the side of the building and into the back yard. Past that was the bushland, and I strolled this way and that as I wound through the eucalyptus trees, stepping over small, fallen branches.

I often walked this way with Mr Buttons, of a morning when we both walked Sandy. I sat on a fallen branch that was set close to a stream of water, and listened to Pobblebonk frogs croaking. One large such frog was sitting on the edge of the water, and I watched it for a while, as it, in turn, appeared to watch me with its bulging, yellow-rimmed eyes. The air was still, and the frogs were the only sounds I heard, apart from the occasional screeching of the yellow-tailed, black cockatoos, an eerie, high-pitched sound that always, for some reason, chilled my blood.

I thought about Cressida. She was always so full of life, so loud. She wore too much make up, and dressed like a theatrical teenager instead of a woman in her fifties or sixties. I looked out at the creek, but my vision blurred and my eyes stung, as warm salty tears welled.

I stayed on the tree branch until I was sure I would not cry again. I had to go back past the boarding house, and I did not want anyone to see me. Finally, after half an hour or so, I stood and turned. My heart leaped into my throat when I saw Dorothy walking my way. She, in turn, seemed just as alarmed to see me. Her head snapped up and she shoved her hand into her coat pocket, but not before I saw she was holding something.

"Oh, didn't know anyone was out here," Dorothy said, her tone snappy.

"I come out here sometimes," I said.

Dorothy simply nodded and hurried past me. I shrugged and walked past the woman, heading towards the bushland that led back to the boarding house. When I was in the trees, I looked back.

Dorothy was still there. I saw her pull something from her pocket and throw it into the lake.

CHAPTER 7

"Hello, Sibyl!" Cressida greeted me with a broad grin.

I gasped. "Cressida! What on earth are you doing here? You're supposed to be in the hospital."

"Oh, don't be silly!" She hiccupped. "You know you're welcome whenever there's an event on here. Come on, have a drink."

"Did the doctors say you could come home?'

Cressida shrugged. "I didn't bother to ask them. I released myself on my own recognisance."

She handed me a tall glass of some clear liquid, and I took a sip. As soon as I did, I regretted it—it burned the whole way down my throat. Whatever it was, I didn't think it should be in a glass this big. "What on earth *is* this, Cressida?" I asked, managing to keep myself from passing out immediately.

Cressida gave me a puzzled look. "Oh, some little cocktail. *Death in the Afternoon*, I think," she unhelpfully tried to explain. It sounded more like one of her artworks than a painting.

"What's in it?" I asked again, desperately.

"Just some champagne, and something called absinthe. We have wine if that's not to your taste." She handed me a glass of wine. I considered throwing my cocktail out the window, but couldn't bear the thought of destroying Cressida's garden.

The night wasn't off to a fantastic start, then. That one small sip had already made me uncomfortably drunk, and I wasn't exactly looking forward to long conversations about ghosts. Mr Buttons had invited me here for a dinner at the boarding house. It wasn't a formal celebration of anything, just a nice way to relax and get to know everybody better. He hadn't mentioned that Cressida had escaped from the hospital. Perhaps he hadn't known at the time.

I looked around the room and tried to take it all in. There were the usual suspects, so to speak. Mr Buttons was sitting at the table, sipping wine delicately and keeping an eye on any potential mess.

I hoped that maybe some alcohol would relieve his urge to clean everything, but didn't get my hopes up.

Cressida, obviously, was also in attendance. I had no idea how she had come into possession of complicated super cocktails, or for that matter, how she had discharged herself from the hospital, but I also knew I'd probably be happier not finding out at all. She was busying herself talking excitedly to some of the ghost hunters.

They were all here, too. Alex was sitting silently alone, ignoring everything happening around him. I assumed he was still in shock over Sue's untimely death, and it was hard to blame him. I'd seen more murders than the average police officer, and I sure wasn't starting to get used to it.

James and Ken were talking with Cressida, or rather, Cressida was talking at James and Ken. Looking hard enough, it seemed as though they were actively trying to stop their eyes from glazing over. They'd nod occasionally and react just a little bit too slowly to any prompting from Cressida, as though she'd asked a question and they only realised after several seconds.

Finally, Michael was sitting opposite Mr Buttons, although he seemed to be admiring the architecture of the building rather than conversing. I followed his gaze, and understood how somebody who hadn't seen this room as often could be so distracted by it.

The table was long—long enough for all seven of us to sit at comfortably, with space for even more guests—and made of polished cherry wood, which reflected the light of the chandeliers beautifully. There were several candelabras scattered along the table, flames dancing softly, casting a soft light that beautifully accompanied the warm electric glow from above.

It was, however, undeniably musty. It was a large boarding house, and was simply too much for such a small staff to manage. I always thought it added to the charm, though, and somehow made it more authentic. I'd visited older houses like this before, but they'd always either been too modernised or too unkempt, losing the charm that the boarding house seemed to display so well.

I sat down opposite Mr Buttons, next to Michael. It wasn't my first choice of seating arrangement, but if I'd walked the whole way around the table I suspected it might seem rude.

"Hello, Sibyl. Glad you could make it." Mr Buttons said earnestly, greeting me with a smile.

I thanked him and smiled back. "Glad to be here. Are you both having fun so far?" I asked both Mr Buttons and Michael. Michael cleared his throat and looked away, so I turned to Mr Buttons for an answer.

"Cressida has been showing us her, ah, art," he explained grimly. As soon as he said it a crack of thunder sounded outside and I heard sudden heavy downpour of rain. I felt a chill run down my spine and took a drink of wine.

"What was that?" Cressida asked, looking up at us. "Did you want to see more art?"

"No!" the three of us yelled in unison, but Cressida had already hurried out of the room to get it. Suddenly, a *Death in the Afternoon* didn't sound so bad.

"What do we do?" I asked in a strained whisper.

"I'm getting out of here. Tell her I'm in the bathroom," Michael announced, standing up.

I grabbed his wrist and held it as hard as I could. "If you go, she'll wait around with it until you get back!" I hissed. "You're just prolonging it for us all. Sit down."

Michael obeyed, taking a seat and looking like he was about to cry. I couldn't blame him. Maybe I could just leave and say I wasn't feeling well.

"Here it is!" Cressida announced from behind me. I saw the colour in Mr Buttons' face drain as he saw it, and slowly turned to see it for myself.

There weren't words in any language from throughout the history of humanity for what she'd painted. It was as if she'd looked into another, darker dimension and pulled back some unspeakable horror.

"I call it *Into the Light*," Cressida announced happily. The entire room was speechless. At that moment, a loud crack of thunder sounded out at the same time as a flash of lightning blinded us, resulting in everybody present screaming simultaneously.

The lights cut out, and we were left sitting in the candlelight, staring at the painting. I hadn't thought it possible, but it had become even more disturbing. "Please put it away," James asked, sounding as though he was about to scream.

Cressida shot him a hurt look.

"You don't want it to be damaged. What if you put it down and somebody steps on it?" I offered, hoping to deflect some of the blame upon James while making sure the painting was moved away.

Cressida smiled wanly and then walked out of the room, and I heard Mr Buttons sigh with relief. I took another sip of wine, being careful that my trembling didn't cause me to spill any. I thought that Cressida should really sell the business and start working in horror films, but decided she'd just take offence at the suggestion.

"What is happening down here?" Dorothy demanded as she entered the room. "Why are you people always screaming?" Her voice was filled with anger. She exchanged a quick furious glance with James, who stared back with equal animosity.

"There was a painting," Ken explained with a tremble in his voice. Dorothy's jaw dropped and she backed out of the room without a word, clearly knowing exactly what had happened. For a while I worried that she wouldn't have the courage to come back out with the food once it was done.

Cressida strolled back out into the dining room empty handed, met with our collective sighs of relief. I was feeling more than a little on edge, and the lights going out hadn't helped. After seeing what was possibly the scariest painting in my life—a statement that was true every time I saw one of Cressida's works—I didn't particularly want to be trapped in a conversation with ghost hunters at all, much less in the dark.

There was another flash of lightning and crack

of thunder, making us all jump. Rain pelted hard against the windows and the candlelight flickered furiously. I wondered what could be causing it to flicker so much, as I couldn't feel any wind. I shivered and pressed in closer to the table, noticing that nobody else looked exactly comfortable either.

"I hope you brought some cameras," I half-jokingly said to Michael, who barely seemed to acknowledge me. He was clearly feeling a bit anxious himself, and I couldn't help but wonder if ghost hunters should be a little braver in the face of this kind of thing. Then again, I was telling myself that I was just being silly, so if I really believed in those kinds of things it would probably be that much worse.

We sat for a few minutes of pained silence, broken only by the occasional attempt to start a conversation. Finally, Dorothy appeared again with the food and started plating it up for everybody. I couldn't tell exactly what it was in the dim light, but it looked to be some kind of meat with vegetables. It was nothing especially exciting, but it tasted fine. Actually, it was much better than Dorothy's regular cooking, and I wondered if perhaps she was improving. Or maybe she was just starting to hate us less.

"Ah, whoops," Ken said, startling everybody. "Sorry, just dropped some in my lap."

Mr Buttons leant down and wordlessly began to rub Ken's leg.

"What are you doing?" Ken demanded as he shot up out of his seat.

"Oh, hold still. I'm cleaning you off. You've made a mess of yourself." Mr Buttons explained, continuing to wipe the food off Ken's leg.

Ken sat back down awkwardly and went back to eating. It was one of the strangest experiences of my life, sitting there in flickering candlelight, eating something I could barely see with an almost completely silent group.

Finally, Cressida broke the silence. "Is this the kind of environment you see ghosts in?" she asked, making me all the more on edge.

"Yes," James said, clearly opting not to explain further.

"Why is that?" Cressida pressed, apparently either extremely interested or just trying to make the meal less awkward.

"Well, there are a few reasons and theories," James explained, setting down his cutlery and clearly settling in for a lengthy explanation. "One of the most common is that electricity, such as in lights, can interfere with our EMF readers. Many also believe that spirits are scattered by UV rays—in much the same process that causes sunburns to us—which is one reason that so many opt to investigate at night and in the dark."

Cressida, Mr Buttons, and I were all listening intently. It was something I'd long wondered.

James cleared his throat and continued. "Another reason for night-time investigation is simply silence, though that matters less here in the country. In cities, investigations need to be done well after midnight, or the sound of traffic and people can interfere too much. We do, however, try to keep the environment as similar as possible to how it was during the initial sighting. If a spirit has only ever manifested in daylight, we'll investigate during the day."

Cressida nodded furiously, following every word. "Isn't it a bit, you know, scary?" she asked. It was a fair question. I was feeling anxious here, with candlelight, surrounded by people. Plus, I wasn't even hunting ghosts, and I knew the boarding house quite well.

"Not when you're as experienced as I am," James said coolly, and I had to stop myself from rolling my eyes.

"It's a good point, though," Michael added. "It certainly makes for more atmospheric and compelling footage, even if not much happens. Try selling footage of a door move slightly in the middle of the day." He laughed.

I looked around and shuddered. It might not be good for their business, but I couldn't wait for daylight.

"I feel sick!" Cressida suddenly announced out the blue.

"No wonder!" Mr Buttons exclaimed. "I have already lectured you about leaving the hospital against the doctor's orders. Now I'll have to take you straight back there."

CHAPTER 8

There was a knock so soft at my front door that I almost didn't hear it. I was standing in the kitchen, leaning against the countertop and eating from a bowl of oatmeal that I held in one hand. I sighed and glanced at the clock. It was a little after seven, and I thought that was too early for anyone to be bugging me.

I kept my bowl in one hand and passed through the living room and to the front door. I opened the door to find the head ghost hunter on my step.

"James, what can I do for you?"

"Oh my goodness," the man said in a dramatic tone, stepping forward. "I feel them. May I come in?"

I hesitated, remaining in front of the man so he

was barred from entering my home.

"You feel what, exactly?"

"Spirits," James said, but his voice was soft, and his attention seemed to be far away.

"There are no spirits here," I said firmly. "You came to tell me my home was haunted?"

James shook his head. "No, I came to ask you something, but I'm telling you, I feel them here. Truly. I would love to come in."

I sighed and stepped out of the way.

James walked directly to the centre of the room. He stretched his hands out and spun slowly. "I wish I had brought my equipment," he said. "This feels like ghosts."

"Who you gonna call?" Max said, and James opened his eyes and glared at the cockatoo.

"I get that from enough humans. I didn't think I'd have to hear it from a bird."

"You'd be surprised what you hear from that bird," I said, closing the door and taking another mouthful of oatmeal.

"Really, I have to come back here later, and bring my equipment. Someone is here. More than one, I think."

I let out a long sigh. "What did you need to ask me?"

"Oh, yes," James said, clapping his hands together. "I was wondering if I could have you come back down to the boarding house with me. I have my camera set up, and I wanted to interview you."

"Me?" I asked. "Why?"

"Well, I know some odd things have happened here, or rather, at the boarding house. And, you know, losing poor Sue. Strange goings-on have been happening, and I'd like to ask you about some."

I pursued my lips. "Look, it's not strange in a paranormal sense," I said. I took my bowl into the kitchen and laid it in the sink. When I returned to the living room, James was by the front door, his hand resting on the knob.

"Please, just agree to come up to the boarding house. I'd like to speak with you and Mr Buttons together."

"Fine," I said. "Give me some time to get ready."

After he left, I turned and headed to my small bedroom. I dressed quickly in jeans and a sweatshirt. I pulled on some white cotton socks on and my old trainers. James was nowhere to be seen, and I guessed correctly that he was waiting for me outside.

Max called after me as I shut the door, "What, no goodbye, you old hag?"

I rolled my eyes and the door clicked shut, and then James and I fell in step with one another and started on the path to the boarding house.

"How did you get into ghost hunting?" I asked as we walked.

"Fell into it, I guess you could say," James said with a shrug. He stuffed his hands into his pockets. "I was always interested in the paranormal as a kid," he continued. "My Grandma died when I was young. She lived with us, and every time I went into her room after that, I could feel her there, with me."

I looked at the man. He looked as though he believed what he was saying. "I'm sorry about your grandmother," I said.

James nodded and then smiled. "Thanks. But like I said, it was a long time ago, and knowing that she was still with me, in that room, it made it all easier, you know? I know we don't stop existing when we die. I know she was there in that house. She wanted to check on me, to make sure I was okay, so she stuck around. I would do it for my grandkids. I will some day."

"You have kids?" I asked, realising that despite

the fact he and his crew had been here for several days already, I knew next to nothing about James.

The ghost hunter shook his head. "No. At least, not yet. I was almost married, but we called it off before the wedding."

"How come?"

"Just wasn't working out. She wanted something different out of life than I did."

"That happens sometimes," I said, as memories of my own bitter divorce flooded back.

"Yeah, she wanted to know that we weren't going to be homeless, and I wanted to prove to everyone ghosts exist. There isn't much money in that, or at least, we thought so at the time."

I couldn't help but laugh. Spending a little time one on one with James had certainly softened my view of him. He seemed strange with his team, and the cameras and the odd tools of his trade. He had been running around the boarding house with the energy of a toddler.

We arrived at the boarding house and went up the stairs to the front door. James pushed the heavy door open and stepped inside, and I followed him. We met Mr Buttons in the dining room.

The dining room was long and rectangular, and its long table had been pushed to one side of the room. James and his crew had set up some filming equipment at one end of the room. I saw a camera, and two lights on metal stands. A love seat was sitting in front of the camera, and the small folding chair was beside it.

"I wanted it to be like a conversation," James said as he moved to the big camera and began to fiddle with it. "Please, have a seat."

Mr Buttons and I sat on the loveseat, and we grinned at each other. I watched as James got the big camera running, and then he moved to a black bag on the floor and pulled out another camera, this one smaller. He pulled out a thin, metal rod which had three bars which folded down to make a stand. He pointed the smaller camera at the empty chair and began recording.

"You all set?" he asked, and we nodded. "Great, we're recording everything, and I can edit it later, so don't worry, be natural."

There was a moment of silence and then James started. "Sibyl, how long have you lived here?"

"Well I don't live here; I live in the cottage on the property, a quarter mile away."

"Right," James said, and I could see he was already flustered. I wondered why he didn't have the other members of his crew there. He didn't appear to be too comfortable with interviewing. "I meant that. How long have you lived in the cottage?"

"A few months," I said.

"Mr Buttons, how long have you lived here?"

Mr Buttons smiled. "Please, call me Thaddeus," he said in an exaggerated English accent.

I had to bite my lip and stare at the floor to keep from laughing. I knew that Mr Buttons' first name was not Thaddeus.

"Thaddeus, how long have you lived in the boarding house?"

"Three years last month," he said, and this at least, was true.

"Have you ever seen anything strange in this house?"

"I've seen a number of people murdered," Mr Buttons said.

"But have you seen anything supernatural?"

"No."

"Surely, in a place like this, you've heard strange noises."

"No," Mr Buttons said firmly.

Once again, I hid my smile. I shot a glance at James and couldn't help feeling a little bad for him. I had been prepared to give him a hard time as well, but my walk over to the boarding house with him had changed my opinion of him, if only a little. I still thought someone who dedicated their life so relentlessly to trying to get a ghost on a recording was a bit daft, but he seemed like a nice guy.

James turned slightly on his fold out chair to look at me.

"What about you, have you seen anything supernatural? Or heard anything?"

"I haven't," I said softly, wishing I could spare his feelings, but unwilling to lie.

"Can I tell you about what brought me here?" James asked, and Mr Buttons and I nodded. "I heard a story about this place," James continued, "and tell me if this brings back any memories of something you might have forgotten, but I heard the tale of a man who died in the attic. I don't know how he died, or why he was in the attic, but he passed away up there sometime in the thirties, and since then people have heard footsteps. A lot of people claim this; I read it all on the internet. You've never heard footsteps?"

"I'm not upstairs enough to hear them," I said. I didn't have the heart to say on camera that the boarding house had no attic.

"I've never heard them, but I am quite old of course," Mr Buttons said, winking at me. "I might be missing it. Perhaps it's time for a hearing aid."

"Maybe," James said. He turned off the cameras and then shook our hands. "Sibyl, thanks so much, and Thaddeus, thank you for the interview."

"Of course. Good luck with everything," Mr Buttons said, and then he and I went out of the dining room.

"Sibyl," Mr Buttons said, "let's take a stroll around the grounds."

"Sure, *Thaddeus*," I said, and Mr Buttons chuckled. We went out the front door and walked slowly down the steps of the porch. We walked along the front of the boarding house and then turned to walk down the side. The back yard was massive and sprawling, and when the manicured lawn stopped, a stretch of bushland began.

We walked in comfortable silence until we were in the trees, and then Mr Buttons broke the silence.

"What about James? Do you think he's the murderer?" Mr Buttons asked.

I took a moment to reflect on it. Finally, I shook my head. "He doesn't quite seem the type to me."

"Is there a type?"

"For murderers? Probably."

Mr Buttons nodded. "You might be right."

"What about Dorothy?" I asked, and then I slapped my forehead. "Oh, I completely forgot. I was walking down here yesterday, and I saw Dorothy throw something into the creek."

Mr Buttons' eyes widened. "What was it?"

I shrugged. "No idea, I was too far away. But why would she throw something into the creek?"

Mr Buttons rubbed his chin. "It would be easy for her to inject poison into hair dye. She had opportunity."

"But what about motive?"

"You've been watching too many crime shows again, Sibyl."

I laughed, but then sobered. "You know, my whole life feels like a crime show these days."

"I don't know what her motive could be," Mr Buttons said, "but clearly, whoever did it had a motive."

Mr Buttons and I walked to the ridge above the creek. The water was murky and green, and small birds darted in and out of the reeds. The sound of the Pobblebonk frogs was ever present.

"I don't know who else it could be," I said, after a few moments. "It can really only be Dorothy,

James, or one of the other ghost hunters for that matter. They knew Sue, but then again, it sounds as if Dorothy and her son, Frank, knew her too."

Mr Buttons nodded, and then we were silent again, both of us working on the same problem. We finally gave up and walked back towards the boarding house. I stopped at the front porch and watched Mr Buttons climb the steps and disappear inside, before I went down the path to my cabin. I pushed the door open and was greeted by the bird.

"Feed me, %$&," he said. I went to his cage and opened a small hatch near the bottom. I pulled out his food bowl and filled it with seed, and then put it back. His water was good but I topped it up, hoping this would redeem me in the bird's eyes.

"Thanks for nothing, you ^%$#@ &##," the cockatoo squawked, and I knew I hadn't redeemed anything. I turned and went to the living room, sitting on the couch and pulling an afghan blanket over my legs. I tilted my head back and closed my eyes, planning on putting some more thought to the task of solving the murder, but instead I fell asleep.

CHAPTER 9

"Are you sure that the lettuce was washed thoroughly?" Mr Buttons called from the dining room.

"Everything's good." I smiled and shook my head as I tossed the salad. Mr Buttons had been agonising over the details of the dinner for most of an hour. I had tried to assure him multiple times that the guests were bound to be glad simply for a nice hot meal. Despite my best efforts, I eventually had to send him to set the table so I could move in the kitchen without tripping over him.

"How about the sauce?"

I sighed. "Just stirred it."

"The pasta?"

"It's all under control." I had grown

accustomed to Mr Buttons' need to micromanage things. I could imagine him in a chef's hat barking instructions at staff.

"I'm sorry if I'm being a bother, Sibyl," Mr Buttons said, as he hurried through the door to check the sauce, wiping the oven surface with a washcloth to clean away any tiny drops of sauce, whether real or imagined. "That confounded woman doesn't let anyone near the kitchen. Thank goodness it's her day off. This is a novelty, albeit a messy one."

"Not at all. It's nice to cook under instruction. Who knows, I might pick up a thing or two."

"We can only hope," Mr Buttons muttered under his breath. "Should we use the linen napkins?" he asked in a louder voice.

"Paper would be better, I think." I knew Mr Buttons normally would not consider paper napkins, but in this case, we were dealing with the ghost hunters and had no idea of their table manners. Further, we were serving spaghetti and garlic bread.

Before Mr Buttons could argue the case for a nicer table setting, the sound of a small crowd echoed down the hall. I pulled a package of napkins and placed them on top of the plates as Mr Buttons rushed past me.

We exchanged a round of greetings as I set the salad and Mr Buttons hurried to finish his place settings. It was not long before we had the group settled in and eating.

"I can't remember the last time we had a real meal," Michael, one of the ghost hunters, said. He leant over and jabbed their leader with a finger. "Hey, James. I promise no one is going to steal your plate. Slow it down before we get traumatised by Alex doing the Heimlich manoeuvre on you."

"Why would Alex be the one?" James asked, wiping a mess of spaghetti sauce off his face, while at the same time fighting a losing battle to get a mass of noodles the size of a baseball in his mouth.

Michael simply rolled his eyes. Typically, Alex remained silent.

"Let me get some more of these for you," Mr Buttons said as he collected the discarded paper napkins, and wiped off a pasta blob that had escaped onto the table. I refilled two wine glasses, while James, Michael, and Ken ribbed each other over dinner.

"My goodness, Sibyl, I've seen better table manners from wild hyenas," Mr Buttons whispered as he threw the napkins in the trash. "Don't they teach basic etiquette anymore?"

"Obviously not," I said, trying not to smile at Mr Buttons' expression of shock and horror.

Mr Buttons washed his hands and gave me a long suffering look.

"Look on the bright side," I said. "The tablecloth is vinyl."

"I don't know if I should be celebrating your foresight, or lamenting it." Mr Buttons armed himself with a washrag, and stuffed a second in his back pocket for reinforcements.

"Well, we won't be washing pasta sauce out of Cressida's starched linen tablecloths," I whispered as we walked back into the dining room.

The group seemed to have settled into eating now that their initial excitement had calmed somewhat. I looked around the group of four men. They seemed nice enough, normal even. It was hard to see one of them as a murderer. Yet, my only suspects were the four men before me, as well as Dorothy and her son, Frank.

"How are you guys doing?" I asked as I set down the drinks, watching Mr Buttons flit around the table cleaning up napkins, and then adjusting the symmetry of the tableware.

"I'm perfect, thanks," Ken said between mouthfuls of garlic bread. "My compliments to the chef."

"Well thank you very much." Mr Buttons stood up straight and smiled. "Sibyl and I make a pretty good team in the kitchen, I dare say."

"You guys made dinner?" James asked as he scooped up a small mountain of noodles and transferred them to his plate.

"That we did," Mr Buttons said proudly, seeming to have forgotten his aggravation as he basked in the praises. "Oh, it was no trouble, really. I certainly enjoyed it."

"That explains why it tastes so good," James said. "I was sure when we came into spaghetti that we were going to be choked on garlic and pepper."

Michael nodded. "And semi-raw meatballs."

"Begone, foul beasts. Back to the shadows of fast food and delivery pizza from whence you came," Ken said dramatically, brandishing his fork at James like a cross in a bad horror movie. James hissed and pretended to shrink away.

"You've been harassed by the cook?" Mr Buttons asked. "You should have said something. It would have been dealt with."

James waved one hand in the air. "We're used to

it. You have to roll with it in our line of work. We aren't popular with some religious circles, despite being faith-based paranormal researchers."

"Most of them are nice enough," Ken said. "There are just some extra hardcore nuts out there who think it's their mission to harass people different from them."

"That woman is as nuts as they come," James said with open distaste, getting surprised glances from his more laid back crew.

"I'll have Cressida talk to her," Mr Buttons said.

I was horrified that Dorothy was causing them so much trouble. I knew the woman had disliked the fact that the ghost hunters were staying, and she disliked the fact that they were investigating. Still, I had no idea Dorothy would be so unprofessional.

James gave him a thin smile and shook his head. "Trust me. I've dealt with her brand of crazy all my life. It would just be kicking a hornet's nest. No telling what kind of drama you'd get mixed up with."

Michael agreed. "Bad vibes. We've seen worse anyway. In one town we had this one person try to sabotage our equipment."

"My poor monitors," Ken said. "They poured soda on two thousand dollars in thermal imagers and HD motion cameras. Like those can be replaced at Target or something."

"Yes, Sue had a fit over that one," Ken said, before his face fell. The four hunters gazed back down at their food, their good humour clearly drenched by the memory of recent events.

"I'm sorry, we should have asked before." Ken looked over at me with a saddened expression. "How is Ms Upthorpe?"

"They say Cressida will be fine soon." I smiled at him. "I'm sorry. I wish it was the same for Sue."

James reached across and patted Ken's arm. "Sue wouldn't want us crying over her."

Ken stabbed a tomato and studied it on the end of his fork. "It doesn't make what happened to her right, though."

"Was she with your group long?" I asked.

"She and James actually started our team," Ken said.

James nodded and then sighed deeply. "We've known each other since grade school. She and I started the group right after high school, though we didn't get serious about it until about half way through college. We had dated off and on all through then."

"They were better off than on, though,"

Michael said, earning him an annoyed look from James. "Well, you were. Every time you two got together, it was constant fighting. You guys were awesome together as boss and manager. Not so much as a couple."

A forced smile crossed James's face. "Fair enough. We made better friends than a couple. It was us against the world, or so it felt. It was a complicated relationship."

"Do your folks still blame her for turning you to the Dark Side?" Ken asked as he dabbed the corner of his mouth with a paper napkin.

"I don't want to talk about them." James rose from the table. "I'd better go over the readings. See you guys in a while. Thanks, Sibyl, Mr Buttons. Thanks for the meal. It was awesome."

I watched James make his way towards the stairs. Mr Buttons almost pounced on the sauce covered plate and half empty glass to clear them away, and he scooted towards the kitchen.

"Now you did it, Ken," Michael said, his voice filled with concern, as he watched their leader retreat. "Now he's going to be broody the rest of the night."

"I'm sorry. I wish I could do something to help,"

I said, earning some fleeting smiles from the remaining trio.

"It's all right. We're all on edge because of what happened to Sue," Michael assured me.

I looked at the three of them. "Do you know anyone who might have wanted to hurt Sue?"

Michael shrugged. "No, not Sue of all people. Most people who didn't like our job at least liked her. She could make friends with almost everyone. She usually did damage control when we met up with groups who didn't like what we do."

"Other than that horrible Dorothy," Ken said. "Sue tried really hard to be nice to her, too. I don't know why she was so nasty. But she really is a hateful old bat."

"Ken!" Michael poked him in the ribs. "Shush!"

"Well, she is," Ken said. "She said we do the devil's work."

Michael shook his head. "She's harmless enough. Not much different from others we've met along the way, right? No need to call anyone names." Michael turned to me. "Sorry. Ken doesn't mean to badmouth the staff. It's just been a hard week for all of us, losing Sue. She was as close to an angel as they come. No one would have wanted to hurt her. There's probably another explanation. Who knows?"

The three thanked me for the meal and went to hunt down their companion.

"Well now," Mr Buttons said from the doorway, looking no less troubled. "What are you thinking about this?"

I shrugged. "We're no closer to finding the suspect, and until we do, Cressida could still be in danger."

CHAPTER 10

Mr Buttons and I were sitting in my cottage, waiting for the test results. The lab had told Mr Buttons they would phone through the results that morning. We had been waiting for ages, but as yet, there was no word. Mr Buttons decided to do a tarot reading.

"I have a new set of cards," he announced, pulling a blue velvet package from his coat pocket. "It's the Thoth deck."

"Mmm," I said.

Mr Buttons shuffled the cards, a look of concentration on his face. He pulled cards, one by one, and set them on the table until fifteen cards now faced up. "On no, the seven of cups," he said. "That means deception, lying, promises unfulfilled."

I was about to point out that any murder would be surrounded by deception, when Mr Buttons' phone rang. "Don't forget to put it on *loud*," I said.

Mr Buttons answered the phone and set it to *loud*, and put it on the coffee table between us. We both bent over it. "Hello," a disembodied voice said. "This is Malcolm Briggs with FDIS. We ran the tests you sent and found a foreign chemical was indeed present in the hair dye sample."

Mr Buttons and I exchanged glances. The voice continued, "We found a potent parasympathomimetic alkaloid, specifically, nicotine, in the sample."

"Nicotine?" Mr Buttons repeated. "Like the stuff in cigarettes?"

"Precisely," the voice said. "It's far more harmful than the general public realises, especially when absorbed through the dermis."

"Oh, I see. Thank you."

"You're welcome. You will receive an official report of the findings in the mail within ten business days."

Mr Buttons ended the call on his phone and looked at me. "Have you heard of nicotine being poisonous when absorbed through the skin?"

I shook my head. "No, but I don't know anything about it. I'll get my laptop."

I returned with my laptop and opened it on the table between us.

"Who would put nicotine in hair dye?" Mr Buttons asked me, clearly perplexed.

"Someone who knows a little more about science than the rest of the world," I said. The search proved easier than I had expected. I read aloud. "It says here that nicotine is rapidly absorbed, and is one of the most deadly poisons known to humankind."

Mr Buttons peered over at the screen. "That's amazing. I never would've thought that nicotine could be fatal."

"Well, according to this, it definitely is. It says that just thirty milligrams—what's that? A third of a teaspoon?—absorbed into the skin can be fatal." I hit the back button and went back to the google list of sites.

Mr Buttons reached across and pointed to the third one down. "Try that one," he said.

"Okay." I clicked the link entitled, *Unflavoured Nicotine Liquid Vapers*.

"What is a vaper?" he asked me.

I shrugged. "No idea. I know as much as you do. Wow, look at that!" I pointed to an image of a bottle on the screen. "Anyone can buy it; those ten milligram bottles are only twelve dollars each, and they are over ninety percent pure liquid nicotine. It would take less than half a teaspoon of the stuff to kill someone."

"A tiny drop," Mr Buttons said.

"Okay, let's find out more about these vapers."

Mr Buttons tapped the screen. "There."

I clicked the link and pulled up an article about the topic. "Okay, it says that *vapers* is the term for people who use e-cigarettes, personal vaporisers, or electronic nicotine delivery systems. Have you ever heard of electronic cigarettes?"

Mr Buttons looked bewildered. "No, I haven't, have you?"

"I did hear something about it a while back on the car radio, but I didn't know what it was. It says here that all three methods of delivery avoid tobacco and use nicotine as their base, along with substances such as propylene glycol, glycerine, and flavourings. This e-liquid is referred to as *juice*, and the consumer chooses their own level of nicotine."

"Well, we found the poison," Mr Buttons said, "and it's readily available for anyone to buy. If one of the ghost hunters, or Dorothy, or her son, Frank, are one of these *vaper* people, then they had the weapon of choice in their hands, so to speak. What do we do now?"

My head hurt from information overload. "Well, if Blake sent the sample to be tested, then the detectives would have the same information by now. I'll call Blake and tell him what we found out, just in case the detectives don't share it with him."

Mr Buttons shook his head. "How do you know the detectives had the sample tested? Blake had to go to Sydney, and the detectives could well have put it on hold. Who knows? I really think you need to call the detectives direct, Sibyl."

I was about to protest, when I saw that Mr Buttons had turned pale. I sighed and reached for my phone.

The call was answered immediately. "Hello, you've reached Detective Roberts," an irritated voice declared.

"Hi, this is Sibyl Potts, from Cressida Upthorpe's boarding house."

"Oh, yes. Is there something I can do for you, Miss?"

"Actually, yes. Mr Buttons and I think that both

of the bottles of hair dye that hurt Cressida and killed Sue were injected with liquid nicotine."

"Nicotine?" the voice parroted with more than a note of incredulity.

I pressed on. "Mr Buttons had the bottle of hair dye that Cressida used tested in a lab, and they found a high concentration of nicotine. Pure nicotine absorbed through the skin is fatal." I took a deep breath. "There is even a syndrome named Green Leaf Tobacco Sickness, which workers get by harvesting wet tobacco leaves without skin protection. Nicotine is harmful to the touch. It's cheap, easily obtainable, and deadly in the smallest of drops."

"I understand your concern, ma'am, but that just seems highly unlikely and rare, if anything. Hold on one moment, please." A few moments of silence followed, and then there was a shuffling sound. "Hey, Henderson. This lady thinks the natural death at the boarding house and the other woman's skin reactions were both intentionally caused by someone using nicotine as a poison."

Laughter erupted in the background. "Like the stuff in cigarettes? I highly doubt it. The doctor even said it was allergies."

"They just won't leave it be. It's bad enough they got that Sergeant to make us investigate."

"It's your call, Roberts, but I just don't think that's likely. Even if nicotine is fatal like they claim, who would know that? I didn't; did you? They don't have any scientists or surgeon generals renting any rooms, so who are we looking at as a suspect if there actually was a crime?"

"That's what I don't know." More shuffling sound assaulted my ears. "Hello?"

"Yes. I'm still here," I said, unable to keep the irritation caused by overhearing their conversation out of my voice.

"Ma'am, do you have a perpetrator in mind?"

"A perpetrator?"

"Yes. If you're so certain that someone is intentionally doing this, it would help to know who you suspect."

"Oh. I don't have a clue."

"That's the problem, ma'am. If there is any actual evidence that can both help us find a suspect and prove that a crime has in fact happened, please do make sure we know about it. Then, and only then, can we take steps to solve this case. I'm sorry."

"Sure you are," I said under my breath as I ended the call.

Mr Buttons patted my shoulder. "Didn't go too well, did it?"

I sighed. "You could say that. I'll call Blake now. He's likely in court, but I'll leave a message." I found Blake in my contact list. Actually, he was on my Favourites list, so I held the phone at an angle so Mr Buttons couldn't see—I didn't want to be teased. I pressed the green phone icon next to Blake's name.

To my surprise, Blake answered at once.

"Blake, it's Sibyl. I thought you'd be in court."

"I'm on a short break. How's everything going? Is Tiny okay?"

I rushed to reassure him. "Yes, yes, Tiny is fine. He's having a good time. Blake, I'm here with Mr Buttons. Mr Buttons took a sample from the hair dye Cressida used, and sent it into a lab for testing, and we've just got the results." I ignored the choking sound on the other end of the line, and continued speaking. "The results showed that pure nicotine was injected into the hair dye. Apparently nicotine is deadly in small amounts when put on the skin, so that's what poisoned Sue and Cressida." Blake's silence worried me, so I added, "About half a teaspoon of the stuff could be fatal, because it's absorbed in such high concentrations through the layers of the skin."

I waited for Blake to speak, and when he did, his tone was none too happy. "So, you and Mr Buttons sent off some hair dye sample to a lab, and found it had high concentrations of nicotine?"

"Yes," I said. "I just phoned the detectives, but they didn't believe me."

Blake sighed. "Sibyl, you should've contacted me before you contacted the detectives."

"But…" I began, but Blake cut me off.

"Sibyl, do me a favour. You and Mr Buttons, stay out of this from here on out."

"But …" I said again.

"I know you want to help and figure out what's going on, but let the professionals handle it. I'll talk to the detectives myself and make sure they start looking into this. Don't worry, Sibyl. I'll make sure we find out what's going on and what happened to Cressida and Sue."

I was frustrated, but he was talking sense.

"Sibyl, I did send the hair dye to the police lab, so I'll call them and get them to send the results straight to those detectives. Just make sure that no one else dyes their hair, and if you find any bottles of hair colour, call Constable Andrews at once."

"Okay, thanks, Blake. I'll tell Mr Buttons what you've said."

"Please do. And Sibyl, I have to make sure it will hold up in court once we do figure it all out. If it eases your mind, I've been dealing with criminals for a long time; they always make a mistake. Before, during, or afterwards, they all make a mistake."

CHAPTER 11

*I* drove my van to dog training. Mr Buttons was sitting in the passenger seat, and the two dogs were sitting in the back. The dogs were excited to be going to dog training—Mr Buttons, not so much.

"Sibyl, I don't want to participate," he said again for the umpteenth time. "I just like watching you and Sandy."

I rolled my eyes. "Mr Buttons, Blake will be ever so appreciative of you taking Tiny to his class. Besides, Tiny is very well behaved, not like Sandy."

As if on cue, Sandy stuck her muzzle forward, and a pile of slobber flew through the air. Mr Buttons whipped out his embroidered linen handkerchief, and I made a mental note to tighten her car harness.

For such a small dog, Tiny's excited breathing was loud. I smiled as I thought once again how strange it was for a big, tall, muscled cop to have a chihuahua. I had enjoyed having Blake's dog with me for a week, and so had Sandy. The dog might have been tiny, but he was as sweet as could be, and tolerated Sandy launching herself on him in glee and playing too rough. He was a tough little dog. However, all this playing happy families had me thinking how nice it would be to have Blake and Tiny with me permanently.

I gave myself a mental slap. What was I thinking? My divorce was new, so new, in fact, that the property settlement was still ongoing. I had an appalling track record with men—after all, my ex-husband had not only tried to kill me, but was delaying the property settlement on the grounds that he was in jail, awaiting trial for the murder of his girlfriend's boyfriend—not to mention my attempted murder of course. I figured that alone and single was the place I needed to be.

I parked the van, clipped the leashes on the dogs, and Mr Buttons and I walked over to the grounds. I nodded to the advanced class. "There you go. Tiny knows what to do."

"But I don't," Mr Buttons muttered as he walked away, with Tiny trotting politely beside him.

I led Sandy to the beginners' class, and she jumped up and down in her excitement. The instructor made us line up. "Now," she said, "make your dogs sit quietly for a few minutes, please." She gave me a long, hard look as she said it. "The advanced class is about to start training on the new obstacle course for the Agility Training competition dogs, and I thought it would benefit you all to watch the first few dogs go through their paces. This is what your dogs will eventually be able to achieve if you work hard enough." She waved her arm expansively.

The advanced class always trained next to us, and I ran my eye over some jumps, some poles, and a big tube. I could see Mr Buttons' face was white and drawn. I gave him a thumbs up, and he smiled weakly.

Mr Buttons' instructor was even louder than mine. "You!" she yelled at Mr Buttons. "You're first. Remember, your dog hasn't done this before, so you need to show your dog what to do first. And remember, this is off leash."

Mr Buttons unclipped Tiny's leash, and took a step forward.

"Stop!" the instructor yelled. "This course is timed! You have to run."

Mr Buttons took off at a decent pace, but to my horror, actually jumped the first jump. Tiny simply ran behind him, but did not jump. My horror increased when I realised that Mr Buttons intended to do the entire course, as if he were a dog. I stood in silence when Mr Buttons ran up and down the steep ramp, and then weaved expertly through a row of poles.

Tiny, so far, had avoided every obstacle. People in my class were chuckling softly, but when people in the advanced class broke into helpless laughter, to her credit, their instructor silenced them. My own instructor was doubled over, shaking and clutching at her stomach.

Mr Buttons had a little trouble jumping through the hanging tire, and even more trouble on the teeter board. Mr Buttons must have been getting tired, as he crashed through the next jump. He righted himself, and then set up the jump again, making sure it was level before he proceeded at speed to the bright blue tube.

I gasped when Mr Buttons disappeared into the

tunnel. I gasped again when he got stuck in the bend. "Help him!" I said to my instructor, but she was in no fit state to do anything. Finally the bulge in the tunnel inched forward, ever so slightly, and after what seemed an age, Mr Buttons emerged triumphantly from the tunnel.

He jogged back to the instructor, who had the presence of mind to congratulate him and act as if nothing untoward had happened. Members of her class, however, did not have such self constraint. Several wiped tears of laughter from their eyes, and several had their hands over their mouths.

"Okay, the show's over! Back to class," my instructor managed to say through her giggles.

I had my mobile phone in my pocket set to vibrate. I usually left it in the van during class, but had been a bit flustered with Mr Buttons complaining at length about taking Tiny into class. We were doing the *Stay*, and my phone vibrated. I resisted the urge to pull it from my pocket as the instructor was staring at me, as she usually did, albeit this time, she chuckled every few moments.

The phone continued to vibrate on and off throughout the class, which was both irritating and frustrating. The second the class was over, I retrieved my phone from my pocket. I did not recognise the Caller I.D., but answered anyway.

"Sibyl," a scratchy voice said.

"Cressida," I exclaimed, before looking up at Mr Buttons, who was hurrying towards me. "It's Cressida," I said to him. "By the way, congratulations on the class."

Mr Buttons beamed.

"Who's with you?" Cressida asked.

"Mr Buttons."

"Well I'm coming home, and I wanted to know if you could come get me."

"Of course," I said. "Let me take the dogs to my place, and then we'll be right there. Sorry I didn't answer first off. We're at dog training."

"All right, but hurry up, will you? I need a cheeseburger. This hospital food is awful."

"Sure," I said. I hung up and slid the phone into my pocket. "Cressida is being released. Do want to come and collect her with me?"

"Yes, and I need a stiff drink after that," Mr Buttons said.

"What, a scotch or something?"

Mr Buttons shook his head. "A Diet Coke," he said in all seriousness.

I laughed as I climbed behind the wheel. I drove to my cottage, and Mr Buttons stayed in the van while I put the dogs in the yard. Then I jogged back to the vehicle and climbed in, a smile on my face the whole time. I was eager to get Cressida back home.

As soon as we walked into the hospital lobby, we saw Cressida and a nurse. Cressida was sitting in a wheelchair, and I figured she wasn't too pleased about that.

"There they are! Can I stand up now?" Cressida asked.

The nurse smiled, a strained smile that told me she was tired of dealing with Cressida, and shook her head. "Not yet, let's get you out through the doors."

"Hurry up then, please," Cressida said through clenched teeth, folding her arms over her chest and leaning back in the chair. The nurse pushed Cressida forward and I held the door open for them. When they were on the sidewalk, Cressida stood and the nurse turned and pushed the wheelchair back inside.

"Good riddance to this place," Cressida said. She then held her arms open and I hugged her, and to my surprise, so did Mr Buttons. Cressida then hurried to the van. "Let's go get that burger; I'm starving."

Cressida sat in the passenger seat while I drove, leaving Mr Buttons to sit in the back of the van. We went through McDonalds drive through, and I ordered a cheeseburger and fries for everyone, with Cressida and me ordering a chocolate milkshake, and Mr Buttons ordering a Diet Coke. As we waited for the food, Cressida leant towards us. "I remembered something about that day, when someone tried to kill me," she said.

"What?" I asked, while accepting the food through the window of my van.

"I saw that ghost boy, Frank?"

"James," Mr Buttons said. "Frank is Dorothy's son."

"Right. I saw James and Dorothy arguing."

"About what?" Mr Buttons asked as I handed him his Diet Coke, and then drove off.

Cressida took a long drink of her milkshake before answering. "I don't know. I don't think Dorothy much cares for talk of ghosts; she seemed mad that James was there. She told him something. I think I'm remembering it right, but she told him there were real things to fear in life, and not to waste his time looking for fake things."

I shook my head. "Real things to fear? That sounds ominous."

"I know," Cressida said, nodding. "It does, don't it?"

Mr Buttons stuck his head into the front seat. "Anything else?"

"It's hazy, to be honest." Cressida shook her head, clearly trying to remember. "Anyway, tell me what's been going on without me."

Mr Buttons and I had visited Cressida in the hospital only the day before, and had told her about the nicotine. Of course, Blake had already informed the doctors. "There's not much to tell," I said. "We brought you up to speed yesterday."

"Wait a minute," Cressida said. "I remember something I thought was very peculiar. Lord Farringdon told me that Dorothy and James seemed comfortable with one another when they spoke. He said it seemed as if they knew each other. I remember thinking it was strange."

"Maybe they do know each other," Mr Buttons said, and I shot him a look. We usually humoured Cressida when she said that her cat provided her with information, but on this occasion, Mr Buttons appeared to be taking her seriously.

"Dorothy's son is the one who contacted James

and his group, telling them about the boarding house. Maybe he didn't just find them online," I said.

"Or maybe he did, but Dorothy knows James as well," Mr Buttons added, "and was upset to see him there."

"I think we need to find out more about your new cook," I said to Cressida, and she nodded.

When we reached the boarding house, I pulled up as close as I could to the steps of the front porch. I helped Cressida up the stairs, even though she kept pulling her arm away and, at the same time, gripping my arm. Mr Buttons followed along with the small bag Cressida had at the hospital, and we took her to her room.

"I don't want to lie in bed," Cressida said, but she lay down anyway, and she quickly fell asleep after I gave her a prescribed pill. Mr Buttons and I left the room, shutting the door.

"Is it safe for her here?" I asked him.

"I can keep an eye on her," Mr Buttons said. "This house has seen some strange things lately, though. I don't know how safe any of us are."

It wasn't a comforting thought. We walked downstairs and sat in the front hall. There were two overstuffed chairs in the rear corner, with a small table between them.

"I wonder if Dorothy is around," I said in lowered tones.

"I think I can hear her banging around in the kitchen."

I nodded and fell silent for a moment. Sure enough, there was someone in the kitchen making noises. Pans banged together, and the water turned on and off. I leant towards Mr Buttons.

"Let's go check out her room," I said.

"Would that be proper?" Mr Buttons asked.

I shrugged my shoulders. "No."

"All right, you sold me on it," Mr Buttons said, slapping his knees and standing up. We crept up the stairs and went down to the end of the hall. Dorothy had the last room on the left, and I felt a wave of relief when I tried the door and it swung open freely.

"Trusting sort of woman," Mr Buttons remarked.

I nodded to him. "Stay by the stairs. If you see her coming up, cough. Loudly."

"Very well." He turned and marched down the hall back to the staircase. I watched him and then went into the room.

Dorothy's room was larger than most of the other bedrooms in the place, save Cressida's. There was a twin sized bed pushed into the corner, and beyond that nothing in the room beside a dresser and a reclining chair. I went to the dresser first, and had just pulled open the top drawer, when I heard Mr Buttons coughing. Surely the woman wasn't coming upstairs, was she? What terrible timing.

I shut the dresser drawer and turned, hurrying for the door. Mr Buttons coughed again just before I exited, and when he saw me, his face relaxed. I pulled the door shut and hurried down the hall. Dorothy and I reached the top of the staircase at the same time.

"Hello," I said.

"Hi," Dorothy replied, in none too friendly a tone.

"Cressida is home."

Dorothy just grunted and brushed past me. Mr Buttons and I watched her walk down to her room and disappear inside it.

CHAPTER 12

Mr Buttons and I were in his car, intent upon investigating Dorothy. It was a quiet car ride, as Mr Buttons did not have his radio on, and the Bentley hummed along peacefully.

I looked at the scenery, all bushland until we reached the mountain, then twists and turns to the bottom of the mountain, after which were green fields and houses dotted here and there, signalling that we were approaching civilisation.

"We'll figure it out," Mr Buttons said, as he turned off onto the exit that led to her first glimpse of civilisation in almost an hour. "I've got your back, Nancy Drew."

I laughed at the nickname. I wasn't planning on

being the local amateur detective who ran after every mystery that crossed my path. I was instead looking forward to a nice, quiet life where the words, *I'm bored,* might cross my mind more than once a day. "Please no. I loved the series, but trouble always found that girl."

Mr Buttons turned his head to glance at me with raised eyebrows. "You're saying it doesn't follow you?"

I had to laugh. "I'm hoping that's a coincidence. I'm serious! No more detective work for me after this one is solved."

Mr Buttons smiled. "Sure, no more detective work, not until the next mystery pops up."

"Stop it, or I'll start calling you my sidekick, George."

Mr Buttons wrinkled up his nose at the idea. "George was a girl."

"It's either that or Bess—and anyway, how did you know that her sidekicks were girls?"

Mr Buttons shot me a look. "I read some crossover stories with the Hardy Boys. Look them up—super mystery series. My mother was convinced that television was out to rot our brains. We spent a lot of time reading and outdoors."

"Did you ever try to solve a neighbourhood mystery?"

"What fan hasn't?" He laughed. "The old man at the corner of the street was very generous about not pressing trespassing charges. It took me a while to learn that not every cranky man who lives alone at the end of the street is hiding a sinister mystery. He was just a hoarder who had a thing for taxidermy."

I laughed, trying to imagine Mr Buttons as a child, sneaking around and peeking in people's windows, looking for adventure. "Now, back to business. Do you really think we'll find out anything from Dorothy's last employer?"

Mr Buttons stroked his chin with one hand. "I honestly don't know, but it's certainly worth a try. It's difficult given that her last place of employment was as a cook in a private hospital. We might've discovered more from a private employer."

I nodded. I had been thinking the same thing. "Still, as you say, it's worth a try."

"It's our only lead," Mr Buttons said. "I'm glad Cressida is staying in your cottage today with instructions not to open the door to anyone. I'd be dreadfully worried if she was alone in the house with that, with that, that woman!" he spat.

The small, private hospital appeared nice enough once we managed to find it after navigating a maze of small streets. The whole hospital was pristine, as I suppose, would be expected. The office windows sparkled. The floors were immaculate, and the décor looked as if it were straight out of a box. Nothing was out of place. The woman at the reception desk directed us to the Human Resources office.

There, at an oversized desk, sat a woman reading a stack of papers from over her glasses. We exchanged handshakes and pleasantries.

"I suppose it's not a surprise that Dorothy took to a boarding house. She was a dedicated cook." The woman wiped her glasses clean as she studied us with a well practiced, friendly smile. Something about the smile felt to me insincere.

I likewise plastered a friendly smile on my face. "Did Dorothy have a lot of contact with the patients?" I glanced down at the copy of the resume I had brought, tilting it so the woman could see it. Mr Buttons had proclaimed that it would make our mission there appear more authentic, and I could see that he was right.

"No, she was a cook. She remained in the kitchens."

I widened my smile and tapped the file. "Is it okay to ask why she resigned her position here two months ago?"

"I'm afraid she didn't disclose that information."

"That's a shame," Mr Buttons said in a pleasant tone with a smile that did not reach his eyes. "Now, as we said on the phone, we happened to be in the area today, so we thought we'd call here in person rather than speak on the phone. We have several applications for the position of cook, but have narrowed it down to Dorothy and one other candidate."

The woman nodded.

I pressed on. "And the reason why we wanted to ask you face to face, is that written references are often glowing, but we need to know the facts. You see, although the position is for a cook, as it is a boarding house, the cook will come into regular contact with guests, so we need a cook who will be pleasant to the guests."

The woman looked down at her desk, and then up at me. "Do you mean you want a people-person?"

I nodded. "Exactly. Is Dorothy a people-person?"

The woman hesitated for a moment before answering. "No. Not at all, actually. In fact, she had a terrible temper." The woman faltered again.

"Do go on, please," Mr Buttons said. "I can assure you; this conversation will go no further."

His words appeared to have the desired effect, as the woman then launched into a tirade against Dorothy. "She was the most obnoxious, ill-tempered woman. She screamed at all the staff. Why, one day, in a fit of temper, she threw glasses at another cook and smashed them against the wall. It's a wonder she didn't cause serious injury to the other cook. That's why we had to let her go."

Mr Buttons and I exchanged glances. "Oh, so she didn't leave employment here of her own accord, then?" he asked.

The woman shook her head. "No, not at all. But please keep that just between us."

We assured her that we would, thanked her, and left.

On the way back to the car, Mr Buttons said to me in lowered tones, "So she lied on her résumé, but that doesn't mean she's a murderer."

I agreed. "We do know that she had a bad temper, though, and she might have murdered Sue in a fit of temper."

"What about Cressida?"

I scratched my head. "Perhaps Cressida was an accident—she was using Sue's hair dye, after all."

Mr Buttons agreed. "That does make sense."

The car ride home was consumed with us comparing notes and discussing the fact that Dorothy had a temper, and what this meant for our investigation. By the end of the car ride, we had made no progress.

"So what's the plan?" Mr Buttons asked as he turned his car into the boarding house driveway and headed further along to my cottage.

"All I can do is call Blake and tell him, but he'll be angry with us for looking into it," I said, my stomach muscles clenching at the thought of Blake's reaction.

"It's obviously that dreadful, uncouth woman, Dorothy," Mr Buttons said. "We should ask Cressida to sack her."

I shook my head. "We have no idea, really. We could be wrong about her."

Mr Buttons got out and hurried around the car to open my door. "How could we possibly be wrong? If it were any more obvious, there would be a neon sign over the dreadful woman's head saying, *Here I am; arrest me!*" Mr Buttons gestured dramatically as he said the last part. "Besides, every time I pull a tarot card about her, it's always *The Moon*, and that means deception."

"Mr Buttons, what if we ask Cressida to sack her and it turns out that she's innocent? What if people ask us where she is? Having to say, *We falsely accused her of murder and sacked her,* wouldn't go over too well at all."

"Is that you, Sibyl?" Cressida's voice called from inside.

"Yes, it's only us," I called out, as I unlocked the door. As we made our way inside, two dogs made a mad dash to the door to give us their energetic greeting. I was glad I was taking care of Tiny for Blake while he was out of town. Sandy and Tiny had become firm friends, to the point where they were now inseparable.

Cressida high stepped and stumbled over the two dogs that were doing their best to stay underfoot. They whined impatiently with their tails wagging in expectation. I leant over and gave each one an affectionate scratch behind their ears.

"Certainly lively here," Mr Buttons said, as he closed the door behind him. "Good day, Cressida. How are you feeling?"

I looked up to see Cressida shuffling slowly,

wrapped tightly in a bright orange robe which was enlivened by purple, sequined flowers. Tiny and Sandy scampered off to chase each other around the room.

My brow creased with concern. "Cressida, you should still be in bed."

Cressida smiled, still as pale as a sheet despite the heavy layers of bright makeup. "I can't stand lying around in bed. You'll be pleased to know I was lying on the sofa, watching TV. Anyway, how did it go—did you find out anything?"

"Do you mind if I use the kitchen, Sibyl?" Mr Buttons said, as he made his way there, already knowing the answer. "Can I make you ladies some tea?"

"I need coffee," Cressida moaned.

"Tea is better for the body and soul."

"Coffee is better for my brain and sanity." Cressida gave a small pout and batted her eyes. One eyelash half fell off and dangled at the corner. Cressida did not seem to notice and I thought it best not to point it out.

Mr Buttons smiled. "All right then. Sibyl?" Mr Buttons turned to me.

"Coffee for me too, please." I smiled at his expression. He shook his head in resignation and muttered about uncouth and unseemly Australians preferring burnt coffee beans to an afternoon cup of Earl Grey or Yorkshire. It had been a regular discussion off and on through the past few months. He was doing his best to convert me, and it was working, at least to some degree.

"Okay, so spill. What did you find out? Anything useful?" Cressida asked as she leant forward, her eyes gleaming with barely contained excitement.

I told Cressida everything, and in the retelling, it seemed not as exciting or useful.

"Ken from the ghost group showed up a little while ago," Cressida commented as she reclined somewhat on the sofa, propped up by numerous cushions.

I was horrified. "But Cressida, we said not to let anyone in! We don't know who the murderer is."

"Calm your farm, Sibyl. I didn't open the door to him—we spoke through the closed door."

*Calm your farm?* Where had Cressida picked up that expression? Aloud I said, "What did he want?"

"He was just checking to see if you were here. He wanted to tell us that James had an altercation with Dorothy, and considerable yelling was involved." Her eyebrows rose. "If Dorothy cannot keep her attitude to herself, then she needs to consider a change in career. I didn't mind her attitude so much when I thought she would avoid the guests."

"She'll be gone before you know it," Mr Buttons said as he returned with back in with coffee in each hand.

"You're probably right." Cressida accepted the cup and stared at the contents. She gave Mr Buttons a charming, pleading smile. "Sugar?"

Mr Buttons rolled his eyes dramatically, but seemed more than happy to go and put the sugar into her coffee. "Would you like ten lumps of sugar, or twenty?"

"Thirty," Cressida said with a teasing, regal tone. "Anything less just kills the taste for me, darling."

I smiled with relief. If Cressida was joking around and drinking more than water, she was well on her way to recovery.

"Okay, you two. Play nice while I make a call." I waved my phone at her.

"Do we have to?" Cressida gave a mock, tragic look.

"Yes, we do," Mr Buttons called from the kitchen.

*I don't know what I'd do without these two*, I thought. I walked outside to make the call in privacy—out the front door, that is—if I walked into the back yard, all Blake would hear would be rude cockatoo speech.

To my relief, Blake picked up on the second ring. I explained that Mr Buttons and I had asked Dorothy's previous employer about her, and had found out that Dorothy had a terrible temper and had been let go for that very reason. I glossed over the fact that we had driven to the private hospital to ask the questions in person.

As I had expected, Blake seemed less than thrilled about me investigating. "Sibyl, I thought I told you to be *careful* while I was gone."

My face grew hot. "Of course I was careful," I said. "Mr Buttons and I were simply checking Dorothy's references, as far as anyone knew."

"*Careful* means doing nothing at all until I get back to investigate." He sighed loudly. "What caused you to look into her last job?"

I explained about Dorothy's more hostile than usual behaviour to the ghost hunters, and their complaints about her harassing behaviour towards them.

"Sibyl, she doesn't have a criminal record, and

we have no motive. Did any of the guests say anything about her making any threats? Were there any attempts to harm them physically?"

"Not that I know of."

"Look, I'll be back soon, and then I'll get this case going. Until then, you are to do nothing, *nothing*. Understood?"

CHAPTER 13

"You want to do what?" I screeched.

James smiled as he paced around my living room, studying the shelves and furniture as he moved. "A ghost vigil. Essentially, we just want your permission to stay over and set up our equipment, to see if we find any activity."

"I thought you guys were here to check out the boarding house." I suppressed a twinge of anxiety over the way he was studying the room. I hadn't even given him permission yet, but he looked as if he was already plotting out where his cameras and dials and whirligigs were all going to go.

"Yep. But paranormal activity doesn't always

stay within four walls. There are even reports of ghosts following their host families halfway across the country. In fact, whole neighbourhoods have reported similar paranormal activities. Speaking of which, have you ever felt like you were being watched in here? Weird cold spots? Stuff moving from where you put it?"

"No, I haven't." I crossed my arms and shuddered. I would rather have such creepy conversations about being watched in broad daylight. I'd had too many close encounters with the living to deal with my imagination being driven out of control. "Look, I understand the whole thing with the boarding house, but your rent does not cover poking around my place."

"It would only be for one night," he persisted. "It would make great ratings if we found some activity over here too. You never know, one of the deceased might have had a strong connection to this cottage. We would even compensate you for the intrusion after the contract is finalised."

"Compensate?" I asked. That sounded good to me. "How much, and would you pay in advance?"

James nodded. When he named the figure, I immediately warmed to his idea. "What ratings?" I added. "A contract with whom?"

James squared his shoulders and threw himself, uninvited, into a chair. "A network had already picked up the pilot, and they've offered me a nice contract." His voice shook when he said *nice*, and I wondered just how much money was involved. "They think we'll top all the other ghost hunting shows," he continued, "given that we back our research with scientific measurements and equipment."

"But all those shows have scientific equipment," I said.

James laughed. "Not as good as our equipment, and while they occasionally do manage to record something that might sound like a voice, we have collected considerable data. That is our point of difference," he said firmly, as if delivering a sales pitch.

I took a seat on the sofa opposite him and tried to process the information. I had thought they were just a bunch of guys hunting for ghosts as a hobby, and now I find they are big business involved with major television. "What does this have to do with the boarding house? And my home? You're not saying that you're planning to put us in one of these episodes?"

"You don't sound sold on the idea." James furrowed his brow.

"Of course I'm not sold on the idea, James. I like my privacy."

"Well, the boarding house will be used to it, given the number of times they've been in the papers lately with murders. Besides, Cressida herself said we could film at the boarding house. That's the only reason we booked in."

That came as no surprise. Cressida would agree to almost anything, given the big renovation bills she was facing.

"Well, I suppose you can film here if you want to," I said, thinking of the money which would certainly come in handy. My divorce lawyer was nothing if not expensive. "It doesn't sound so bad. You can point those thermal digital things and take temperatures here if you like."

James broke into loud laughter. "Temperatures and digital things, right?" he said after he managed to stop laughing. "The viewers are going to want more than temperature readings and thermal cameras, Sibyl. They want the story behind it."

Warning bells went off. So, it seemed to me that James was going to bring in the recent murders. Newspapers and local news were one thing. Most people don't check the news archives before selecting a boarding house or dog groomer. After the initial shock, things more or less settle back down over time. Yet, James's ghost series was going to be shown on national television, and that meant that Little Tatterford would likely attract more than its fair share of morbid people nosing around.

"What about poor Sue?" I asked. "Do you really want to do a television show where she died and, I assume, mention her ghost?"

He gave a bit of a shrug, seeming at a loss how to deal with my question. "Her memory would live on, right? And the director liked the idea of trying to contact a lost team mate."

I shook my head. "James, I will allow you to film in my cottage if you pay me in advance, but it's dark outside, and I don't like talking about ghosts after dark." I nodded to the door, and then shook my head. Did James really intend to use his ex girlfriend for ratings? It seemed so.

James took the hint. "Goodnight, Sibyl, and thanks."

I smiled thinly and opened the door.

I screamed as I saw a tall figure on the doorstep, his arm raised. James and the figure both stumbled back at my reaction. As my eyes adjusted to the dark, I recognised an equally startled Blake.

"Nice to see you, too," Blake said, his brow furrowed.

I turned to James, and stepped away from the door. "Good night, James. I'll talk to you tomorrow about things."

James gave us both a gloomy look as he nodded, and walked out the door.

"Is he ghost hunting here?" Blake asked as he closed the door behind him. His tone was jovial, but I could not help but notice an edge to his voice, almost as if he was annoyed that James was here. Before I could respond, Tiny and Sandy both appeared to greet Blake in a whirl of fur and wagging tails. Where had they been while James was around? Come to think of it, they had made themselves scarce right after James had arrived.

"Yes, James was here to ask if he could do a ghost hunting vigil here. He said he'll pay in advance." I knew I didn't owe Blake an explanation, but for some reason, I was a little anxious in case he got the wrong idea. "I didn't expect you until late tomorrow."

"Court wrapped up early around midday, so I was able to drive straight home."

"Were you afraid that Mr Buttons and I were going to do a secret mission without you?"

Blake smiled, and put Tiny down. "I'm surprised the town is still in one piece." He took a step backwards and studied the scenery outside the window for effect, acting as if he were making sure it was in fact still intact. "It *is* still in one piece, right?"

"Nothing some super glue and a reality TV show couldn't fix. Anyway, would you like some hot chocolate? I was about to make myself a comfort drink, once I got rid of James."

Blake smiled at that. "Sounds good, thanks. A week of stale continental breakfasts and coffee flavoured water got old real quick." He picked up Tiny again and gave the wriggling, squirming, happy dog a belly rub while cradling him in one arm. Tiny was the picture of contentment as he lay with his tongue lolling out the corner of his mouth. "Was James giving you a hard time?"

"Let's just say it's been a long week," I said. Had Blake been irritated about finding James at my place at this hour?

"Tell me everything." Blake followed me into the kitchen.

I would have thought, as tired as I was a minute

ago, that talking about the long and strange week would be the last thing that I would want to deal with right now. Yet the instant Blake asked, I felt a wave of relief. It seemed to me that no matter what was going on, everything was going to be okay because he was there.

CHAPTER 14

As we walked into the first room, I saw James and the other ghost hunters tinkering with their fancy equipment, readying it for filming.

"Do you think this was such a good idea?" I whispered to Mr Buttons. "I mean, us asking to join them so we can keep an eye on them?"

Mr Buttons simply shrugged. "It's all we can do, really."

The dining room of the boarding house was crammed with various paranormal equipment. I noticed a small recorder sitting beside a strange device that looked more like a failed retro video game console than any type of ghost hunting item. "What's this stuff?" I asked.

"That's the EVP field processor. Be careful with it!" James scolded me. "Look, but don't touch!"

"What does it do?" I asked.

He shot an annoyed look at me. "It's an EVP field processor," he repeated slowly and carefully, as if speaking to a young child. "We use a digital recorder to ask the spirits questions, and sometimes they reply, but their voices can't always be heard by the naked ear. They can only be heard during playback. This device here alerts us when a foreign noise or sound has been picked up, giving us a better idea of where to look for some proof of communication on the recording's timeline."

"Oh," I said, unexpectedly satisfied with the answer. Mr Buttons and I continued looking at the various equipment that was strewn out around the room: cameras, strange canisters labelled *REM-Pods*, meters, and all the other odd objects that decorated the room, making the whole place feel more haunted than it had ever seemed before.

"Okay, this is how it'll go," James began. "You two, you're here to observe and help us communicate if necessary. Other than that, just pretend you're part of the boarding house."

"We *are* part of the boarding house," Mr Buttons whispered.

I resisted the urge to laugh.

James continued speaking. "You guys, let's just do this the usual way." The other ghost hunters readied their gear. Alex and Michael set up cameras in the room; Ken set up three flashlights in a row, and James kneeled down and opened an impressive looking metal case.

"Hello, hello," James said when he stood up. "Is anyone here? Come forward. Do you want to speak to us? Give us a sign."

Nothing happened. James repeated the words several times, and then, all at once, there was a scratching sound on the closed door.

I gasped and seized Mr Buttons' arm. I looked at the ghost hunters, and the four of them seemed terrified too. I fleetingly wondered why they would ask if there was anyone there, and then be terrified when there was a response.

The scratching sound came again, and by now, Mr Buttons and I were clinging to each other. I wanted to flee, but the only way out was through the door which was currently being scratched by what I assumed was a fearsome entity.

Just then, the door opened, ever so slowly. I gasped in horror. I saw that Alex and Michael had the presence of mind to edge forward, each holding up a small camera. James, for some reason, seemed more scared than the rest of us. I hid behind Mr Buttons, who in turn, was hiding behind a dining chair.

As the door opened wider, I peeked over Mr Buttons' shoulder.

Lord Farringdon walked in.

"It's only that cat," James screeched. "Catch it!"

Lord Farringdon's relaxed demeanour at once changed when he saw James lunging for him. His tail fanned out like a toilet brush and he shot out the door.

I clutched at my throat, and breathed a long sigh of relief. Mr Buttons stood up, still holding onto the back of the dining chair, and I saw that he was shaking.

James came back into the room, minus Lord Farringdon. "I'm going to take the all-vision goggles and go upstairs," he said.

Several minutes later, a commotion erupted. James flew back into the room in a panic, holding his left arm with his right hand. The ghost hunters didn't react in any way other than by making sure they got the shot. We all crowded around as James revealed his arm. Three long, deep marks were etched into his skin. He looked up at one of the cameras and spoke softly, albeit with more than a hint of melodrama. "Something or someone doesn't want us here."

At that point, Michael and Ken stopped filming, and Alex turned on the light. I took a good look at the scratches. They were definitely real. The only question was, were they self inflicted, or had a ghost done it?

James, after complaining about the scratches, once again left the room, leaving the rest of us there. After we had been filming for a little over an hour, I was dreadfully bored and the crew was beginning to get restless. There had been several occasions where James had returned and mentioned that he had seen or heard something out of place, but nothing concrete had as yet happened to affirm the presence of any supernatural entities. "I really don't think we're going to pick anything up, man," I overheard Michael say to James.

"I definitely picked up something in the west corridor," James said. "I'm sure we'll get something in playback. I think we should record some audio in here now." James turned to me. "By asking questions and monitoring the radio waves, we can pick up on communication attempts of a supernatural nature."

I nodded.

"Is anyone here?" James paused and looked intently at the meter he was holding in one hand. In his other hand was the digital recorder. "Are you trying to communicate with us? Do you welcome us, or do you want us to leave?"

Silence was the only response that could be heard. Suddenly, what sounded like a door slamming reverberated through the floor. We all jumped.

James held the recorder higher out into the air. "We aren't here to hurt you. We just want to find out more about you, who you are, how you got here. Do you need help to move on?"

Just then, the most eerie sound came from behind the door. A chill ran down my spine. Mr Buttons and I wasted no time assuming our positions behind the dining chair. We cowered, as high pitch sounds emanated from the corridor.

"There's something out there!" Michael yelled. "Something's broken through the REM pods!"

I didn't know what REM pods were, and I didn't care—yet the fact that something had broken through them seemed alarming.

There was no further sound, so James slowly edged towards the door. He opened it, and Lord

Farringdon was sitting there, looking quite pleased with himself. This time, when James lunged for him, Lord Farringdon ran straight into the dining room towards me.

I picked him up and soothed him. "I'll go and shut him in Cressida's room," I said. "Mr Buttons, will you come with me?"

As we walked past James, Mr Buttons said, "We haven't heard a single peep from a ghost all night."

"That's completely understandable," James said. "The thing is, you often can't hear them without the equipment. We usually wait until we go back over all of the recordings the next day." He pulled out a recorder and fidgeted with the buttons. After a few moments, a recording played. We heard James' voice trying to communicate with spirits.

"Do you welcome us, or do you want us to leave?" his recorded voice asked.

"Leave!" The lone word came out as a raspy, horrid whisper.

James rewound the recording and pressed play once more, and we heard the ghastly sound again.

"That is most creepy and unseemly," Mr Buttons whispered. I nodded in agreement.

Lord Farringdon did not object when we placed

him in Cressida's bed, and then shut him in her room.

On our way back to the dining room, Mr Buttons whispered to me, "Do you think it's all faked?"

"What is faked?" I said. "Nothing's happened so far, apart from that one creepy voice."

"True," Mr Buttons said, "but I don't mind telling you, I'm not comfortable with this."

As we approached the dining room, I could hear a dispute, and the dining room lights were back on. James was speaking forcefully. "I don't understand why you guys are against it. Sue was part of this stuff too. She believed in it, and I know she would want to talk to us if she was able to."

"What?" I asked, as I walked over to them.

"James wants to see if we can communicate with Sue's spirit," Michael said, and Alex shook his head.

James' hands were on his hips. "I just figured we might be able to ask her what happened to her. Maybe she can tell us if this was an accident or if someone caused it."

"Sure, it would be nice to know what happened, but don't you think this is the wrong way to go about it?" Ken asked him.

"It's in poor taste," Michael said.

All four men all looked quite irritated.

Mr Buttons put his hand on James' shoulder. "James, they're your crew, and she was their friend too. Just let them have a say in the matter, at least. No?"

His words of wisdom seemed to get through to James. He nodded. "Look, I won't keep pushing it. Just let me ask once, and see if she answers. If not, we move on and forget about trying again. Does that work?"

Each of the three men looked at each other and then their leader. In unison, they all nodded agreed to his terms. "It's still in poor taste, as far as I'm concerned, "Michael said, "but if it helps at all or at least doesn't harm anyone or anything, I guess it's worth a shot."

"That's all I'm asking for," James replied. He turned to face the centre of the room. "We wish to speak to a spirit named Sue. She was recently lost from this world and delivered to yours. Please break through the barrier and speak to us. We miss you." Silence met his query.

After about five minutes, Michael spoke. "It's just not going to happen, James."

"Why do you think that?" asked Mr Buttons.

"We've just never spoken to recent spirits before," Michael said. "They're always ghosts that have been reported as haunting specific locations for years before we even show up or hear about it. I think James was just hoping to catch something unexpected on camera for this show. It's really important to him, so he might seem a bit overzealous at times, especially during recording. This show is his baby; he is very protective of it and wants it to be the best it can be."

"You can't really blame me for that, can you?" James said.

Michael and Ken murmured agreement, and Alex nodded.

"All right, we're about ready to call it a wrap." James looked down at his watch. "We're going to keep the cameras rolling for the next few hours while everyone sleeps. We might need you two to do some interviews tomorrow."

Mr Buttons and I looked at each other and then at James. "Us?" I said.

"Yes. We like to splice together interviews about the actual events and reactions that we recorded during the investigation. It won't take long—it'll be fun!"

I agreed reluctantly.

"Well, that was an experience," I said to Mr Buttons as we walked out, leaving the ghost hunters behind. Do you think this stuff is all real?"

"I do believe in ghosts, and I do believe that genuine paranormal researchers have discovered valid evidence as to the presence of such ghosts," he said, before pausing for a moment. "I just don't know whether James is for real."

"Yes, that's my problem as well. Plus I'm sure he intends to edit out Lord Farringdon, to make it seem as if a spirit was making those sounds and opening the door."

Mr Buttons turned to me and laughed. "At least we got to see how scared the ghost busters were when Lord Farrington got the drop on them."

CHAPTER 15

Mr Buttons and I stood in the doorway of Sue's room, watching as Sue's cousin, Chloe, put Sue's belongings in a cardboard box. The girl was thin and short, with her long brown hair tied up in a loose ponytail that bobbed behind her with every move she made. She wore an oversized sweatshirt with her name printed across it in big, blocky letters.

When the girl turned to us, I saw tears shining in her eyes, and as I watched, one slid over her bottom eyelid and ran down her cheek, leaving a long line of black mascara over her pale skin.

"I can't believe she's gone," Chloe said.

"I know," I said. "We're all shocked."

Chloe wiped her eyes. "I should get going. It's a long drive back home."

"Why don't you have a nice cup of tea with some cucumber sandwiches first," Mr Buttons said. "That will make you feel a bit better."

Chloe nodded, sending her ponytail in every direction. "That sounds nice," she said.

We gathered in the dining room, the box of Sue's stuff on the oak table in front of and a little to the right of Chloe. Mr Buttons placed a steaming mug, filled to the brim with tea, before each of us, and a plate of cucumber sandwiches, minus their crusts and cut into tiny triangles.

"I knew James was bad news," Chloe said.

"What do you mean?" I asked her.

"Well, he faked it all, of course. Everything, the ghost stuff. I mean, to be honest, we all thought it was silly—Sue's friends and I— but she believed it and she liked doing it, and what's wrong with a hobby, you know? But it was all a joke to James. He faked it. We could tell right at the beginning."

"You could tell?" Mr Buttons said.

Chloe sniffled and nodded. "We watched their videos, and we could tell it was all fake, but Sue just refused to believe it. I mean, she refused to believe he would fake it, not that she refused to believe in ghosts. But we could tell—it was obvious."

I sipped my tea, and then turned to her. "I take it you don't believe in ghosts?"

Chloe shook her head. "No, of course not. I wish I did though, now that Sue has gone. I wish I thought she was with me still, right in this room with us, but I just can't."

I nodded. "Do you think James did something to Sue?" I asked. I hadn't planned to be so forthright, but thought I might as well take the opportunity.

Chloe was silent for a moment. She took a sip of tea, and then shook her head as she placed her cup back upon the saucer. "No," she said finally. "I met him on several occasions. He doesn't seem like that. Well, maybe I'm wrong. Is he here?"

"James? No, they're out filming at some other locations. There are lots of local ghost stories, so I guess they want to check some out," I said. "You know, you're welcome to stay here tonight. It's getting late."

Chloe nodded, but then she smiled and the nod turned into a shake. "I don't think so," she said. "That's nice of you, but Sue died here. I couldn't bring myself to stay here. I really should get going now. I'll finish my tea, though."

"Do you mind if I ask you a few questions?" I said.

"Sure."

I looked at Mr Buttons, and he nodded slightly.

"Had anyone ever threatened Sue?"

Chloe laughed, the first time she had done so since arriving at the boarding house. "No, absolutely not," Chloe said. "Sue was great, everyone loved her. She was a wonderful person."

I persisted. "How did she get into the ghost stuff?"

Chloe shrugged. "You know, I don't really don't know." She stood up. "I should go."

"Thanks for talking with us," I said, standing as well.

Chloe picked up the cardboard box filled with Sue's things, and then she left. I went with her to the door and helped her out, and then I returned to the dining room and sat across from Mr Buttons.

"So James has always been faking it?" Mr Buttons asked.

"Sounds like it."

"Did he kill that girl?"

I sighed and shrugged my shoulders. "I don't know," I said. "I really don't know."

We sat like that for some time, in the dining room, our own cups of tea hardly touched, and the liquid within the cups cooled and still we sat, thinking. We did a lot of thinking together, and somehow it seemed as if we were smarter when we sat silently next to one another. Finally I stood up—the sky was growing dark, and I knew I should get home.

When I got home, the sky was black and the stars were out. I fed Sandy, and then sat on my front porch for a moment and thought about Sue, and I ran through possible suspects.

There was Dorothy, who had a violent temper, and there was James, with his smug face, and the way his eyes never seemed to be open quite enough, as if he were always in the middle of telling a secret. Chloe had seemed to believe that James could not possibly be the killer, but the more I thought about it, the less sure I was.

Finally as the night drew on, I went inside. I went straight to bed, but sleep eluded me. Instead, I thought some more about everything. I tossed and turned for hours before I finally fell asleep.

I had a dream about Chloe, and Sue. In my

dream, Chloe was watching television, a show about ghost hunting, and James was on the screen, speaking to the camera. Behind Chloe, the door swung open, and there was Sue, her face as white as a sheet. Sue was floating, her arms outstretched. She was a ghost in that dream; no one would have been able to mistake that. In the dream, Sue floated to the television and turned it off, but Chloe did not see her.

I sat up in bed and thought about the dream. It was strange. I had never had a dream before that didn't include me. It was as if I was simply part of the audience. It made me uneasy. I knew it was a clue, perhaps as to the identity of the murderer, but what on earth did it mean? Sue turned off the television show about ghost hunting. That was no help at all.

I got up and showered, and then went into the kitchen after throwing on shorts and a long sleeved tee shirt. I made breakfast and ate alone in silence, leaning against the kitchen counter as I spooned up mouthfuls of oatmeal. The dream still weighed heavily on my mind.

After I rinsed the bowl and set it in the sink, I went back to my bedroom to get my mobile phone. I sat on the edge of my bed and scrolled through my contacts until I came to Chloe. As Cressida had been in the hospital when the police had notified Chloe of Sue's passing, they had given her my phone number to make arrangements to collect Sue's things. The number was still saved.

"Hello?" Chloe asked. It sounded as if she was driving.

"Hi, it's Sibyl."

"Oh, hi."

"Are you okay? On the road already, or did you drive straight through the night?"

"No. I stopped, but I got an early start. I couldn't sleep much. I kept having bad dreams."

"About Sue?"

"Yes," Chloe said.

"I had one, too," I admitted, but I didn't tell Chloe that she had been in it as well. "Do you mind if I ask you something?'

"No, go ahead," Chloe said.

"Did Sue ever try to stop James from having a television show?" There was a moment of silence, and I thought that the connection had broken. "Hello, Chloe, are you there?"

"Oh yes, sorry. Funny you should ask, I just remembered that Sue was upset when the network picked up the pilot. She didn't say why."

I was afraid Chloe would ask me why I wanted to know, so I changed the subject. "Thanks. Well, I was just checking on you. Do you mind calling me when you get home so I know you made it all right?"

Chloe laughed. "I will."

"I don't even really know you or anything," I said. "I just…" I didn't know what else to say, so the words trailed away, fading as quickly as they were said.

"I understand," Chloe said. "I'll call you. Thank you."

"Thanks," I said, and then I hung up. I sat on the edge of my bed for a long time, wondering why I had the dream about Sue, and what Sue not wanting James to proceed to with the television show had to do with anything.

CHAPTER 16

"Morning, Sandy. Are you ready for a walk?"

Sandy went into a spasm of excitement at the word, *walk*. She jumped up and down on the spot and twisted this way and that. After I put her leash on her, we walked to the van and were soon heading to the local dog park.

It was a lovely morning. There was a light breeze through the eucalyptus trees, and the bushland smelt lovely and fresh. The cloudless, blue sky hovered over the small town like a cozy blanket and the whole atmosphere made me eager to start the day.

I enjoyed my regular early morning walk in the dog park. Sandy looked forward to it, perhaps even more than I did, and was always eager to venture out. For me, it was the one time during the busy day that I was able to get away from my worries and concerns.

My world had been turned upside down over the past few months, but for now, I was going to relax in the peaceful surroundings of the Little Tatterford dog park.

As I walked along, I had to admit that I missed Tiny, Blake's chihuahua. Now that Tiny was no longer staying with me, the cottage was a lot quieter, but on the other hand, Sandy was less boisterous when Tiny was around. The constant playing with Tiny tired her out. I had enjoyed watching Sandy and Tiny play, and I had enjoyed them snuggling up beside me on the couch. It was clear to me that Sandy missed Tiny. At any rate, I was hopeful I might see Tiny, and with any luck, Blake, at the dog park.

As Sandy pulled at her leash, forcing me to quicken my pace, I realised how much I loved the peaceful country town. Despite the latest events at the boarding house, Little Tatterford was my home, and I wouldn't trade my life here for anything.

Finally, our walk was over, and we were back at the wide, open space just inside the entrance gate. I sat on a large boulder and slipped off Sandy's leash. Sandy, freed from the constraints of her leash, ran wildly after magpies and any other low-flying birds.

Tiny appeared as if from nowhere, and Sandy headed straight over to him. The two rolled around the grass together, clearly excited that they were reunited.

"Hey, Tiny." I said. The thought of Blake being close by made me shiver with nervousness. I looked around in every direction, but there was no sign of him.

"Looking for me?" came a deep, masculine voice from behind.

Blake's tall frame towered above me and I did my best not to stare at his broad shoulders, chiselled features, piercing blue eyes, tanned skin, and white teeth. I found him disturbingly appealing. It was starting to have an effect on me, and I wasn't sure how much longer I could deny those feelings.

I blushed. "I was actually looking for Tiny's owner." As soon as I said it, I thought it a silly thing to say.

Blake smiled. "And that would be me, so I was right, you were looking for me."

I simply smiled in response. "Sandy and Tiny are pleased to see each other."

"Yes, and Sibyl, I wanted to ask you something."

I frowned. "What is it?" At that moment, Sandy ran up to me, slobbered on my jeans, and then ran back to play with Tiny some more.

"I very much appreciated you minding Tiny when I was away, and I'd like to thank you properly. I'd like to take you to dinner tonight."

I just continued to sit, but I was shocked. Was Blake asking me on a date? Or was it simply dinner with a friend, a dinner to thank me for minding his dog?

I sat a while. A gust of wind blew a strand of hair across my face. I could feel Blake's gaze upon me. I did not mean to leave him waiting; I just found it difficult to process the unexpected invitation.

The truth was, as much as I tried to deny it, I was attracted to him. The problem with that was that I was certainly not ready for any form of a relationship. My property settlement was still in process—well, to be fair, it would have all been done and dusted by now if my ex-husband didn't have a fancy lawyer and had made mileage out of being in jail. My last relationship had been such a mess, that I was sure that now was not the time to start dating again.

On the other hand, perhaps Blake simply did just want to thank me for taking care of Tiny. I had to consider the possibility that maybe there was no romantic sentiment behind the invitation. Regardless of the reality, the thought helped me to keep my growing attraction in check.

I rubbed my forehead in the realisation that I was unable to clear my head. One thing was sure, I did want to know more about Blake and I did want to be around him.

"Sure, thank you," I finally said, earning a smile from Blake.

"I'll call for you at seven," he said. "C'mon Tiny, let's go."

I watched as Tiny and Blake jogged away from us, up the trail alongside the gully flanked by a row of silver top, stringybark, eucalyptus trees. I sat there a little longer and thought about Blake's ex-girlfriend. I had never met her, of course, as by all reports, they had broken up over two years earlier.

That evening, I sat on the edge of my bed, staring at my dismal excuse for a closet, while Sandy peered into the closet too, no doubt thinking that dog treats were hidden inside. Soon, Blake would collect me to take me to dinner. I was facing a girl's worst nightmare. I had nothing to wear. My closet was filled with jeans, shorts, and shirts, but no nice dresses.

"Aha," I exclaimed, and Sandy looked up at me expectantly. "I'd forgotten about that black dress I bought online ages ago. I know it must be here somewhere. Now if only I can find it."

I rummaged through my drawers and closet like a mad woman. Soon, garments were strewn everywhere and the room was covered with a blanket of clothes and shoes. Even Sandy was now hidden under a pile of shirts, skirts, and bras.

"Found it," I shouted after pulling a sock from Sandy's mouth. My excitement soon faded when I checked the time. I had exactly twenty minutes to get myself together before Blake arrived. I ran into the bathroom for a quick shower.

Fifteen minutes later, I did not recognise the image in the mirror. The long black dress fitted like a glove and hugged me in all the right places. Furthermore, by some miracle, I had managed to do a flawless job with my makeup. I gathered my purse and sprayed my favourite, and only, perfume on my wrist before snatching up a pair of pearl earrings. At that very moment, there was a knock on the door.

I froze. The rush to prepare had prevented me from being nervous, but now a terrible bout of nervousness hit me all at once. My heart raced out of my chest. Butterflies churned horribly in my stomach.

I adjusted my dress, glanced at my reflection for the last time, and walked towards the door. I took a deep breath before opening the door.

Blake spoke before I could. "Wow, Sibyl, you look stunning," he exclaimed. "You look beautiful."

I felt myself blush horribly. "Err, thanks," I stammered. "You don't look so bad yourself." I then silently scolded myself for saying something so lame.

Blake led the way to his car. He held the door open for me, before making his way around to the driver's seat.

There was silence in the car. My nerves had left me well and truly mute, and Blake appeared to be focused intently on the road. I suddenly felt over dressed, shy, and uncomfortable. Did I think the date was more than what he had in mind? Did I overdo my clothes? Was Blake stunned by the fact that I was so dolled up, that it left him speechless?

Was he thinking it was only a thank-you dinner after all?

We barely exchanged a word in the twenty minutes into Pharmidale, and so I was relieved when Blake turned his car off the highway. My relief was short-lived when I saw that we were heading for Three Orchards, the most expensive restaurant in Pharmidale.

When the hostess led us across the floor of the lavish restaurant, I held my breath with every step. I had never been there before, but I had heard of its reputation. Long, crystal chandeliers provided a muted light. The tables were set with wine glasses, plates, and cutlery of the highest quality. Soft jazz music played in the background, and the restaurant was abuzz with Pharmidale's wealthiest. I could not help but feel out of place.

"Have you ever been here before?" Blake asked, finally breaking the ice, after we were seated at an intimate, corner table.

I chuckled. "No, I haven't. I've heard quite a bit about the place, though. I must admit, I've always wanted to come here, so thank you for bringing me."

"Not a problem." He smiled. "I really wanted to thank you for taking care of Tiny. I could tell he had a great time at your place. He and Sandy make quite a pair."

I smiled, but my stomach churned yet again. Was this Blake's way of making it clear that this was not a date—that he was only taking me to dinner to thank me for minding Tiny?

"And it was good of you to take Tiny to dog training, too," he added.

"That was Mr Buttons," I said. "Perhaps you should've brought him to dinner, too." *And next time, Sibyl, think before you speak*, I added silently.

I need not have been concerned, as Blake clearly considered my remark quite funny. When he finished laughing, he said, "I don't find Mr Buttons nearly as attractive as I find you, Sibyl."

I didn't know where to look. Perhaps this was a date, after all. I really needed Patti Stanger here to explain it all to me. All I could do was stare at my wine glass and hope my face wasn't as beet red as it felt.

After that initial fright, the rest of the evening went by smoothly. We talked about everything from sports to the local wilderness area. The conversation flowed easily, and both of us avoided any mention of the poisonings. At times, Blake had me in tears of laughter with his witty sense of humour, while at the same time making me feel relaxed and comfortable. I could be myself with him, and by dessert, I felt as if I had discovered a whole new side of Blake.

Of course, I still had my reservations. I was still reeling from a painful divorce—I mean, divorces are bad enough, but not everyone's ex-husband tries to kill them—and I wasn't ready to fall in love again. I had a bad track record with men, and I had no intention of making the same mistake, and falling for a man who seemed ideal at the time, only to find out years later that it was all a big blunder.

"I really enjoyed your company tonight, Sibyl," Blake said, as we headed back down the highway to Little Tatterford.

I muttered, "Yes, likewise," in reply. I really did need dating help. For a start, I needed to know whether or not this was actually a date.

When we arrived at my cottage, Blake again opened my door. We walked together the short distance to the cottage, and I took out my key.

"Good night, Sibyl," Blake said.

I looked up at him to say goodbye, and then caught my breath as Blake leant in closer. He was so close, I could smell the subtle scent of his aftershave, and his breath tickled my skin. I took a deep breath in anticipation of Blake's next move. Blake pressed his lips against my cheek in a soft, short kiss.

Then he was gone. I leant against the door, watching him drive away. "Yes, it was a date, after all," I said aloud. "I'm sure he wouldn't kiss Mr Buttons."

CHAPTER 17

It was a few minutes before nine at night, and I was doing a last minute tour through my house, making sure there was no clutter. I had just finished my inspection, when there was a soft knock at the door.

I hurried and pulled the door open, and there stood James, Alex, Michael, and Ken. There were four oversized black bags on the ground at their feet.

I wasn't sure why I had agreed to this. James had cornered me that afternoon, and had asked if his team could come that night at nine to do an all night vigil in my home.

James smiled now and stepped inside, followed by the other three men. "Sibyl, thanks again for having us," James said, and I smiled as best I could by way of response. I shut the door behind them and turned around, watching as each man set a black bag on the floor and took out different tools. There were cameras and strange electronics.

"Would anyone like some coffee?" I said. "Or some Cokes or something?"

"I'll take a Coke," James said. Tony and Michael nodded as well, so I went into my kitchen and pulled some cold cans from my fridge, and then returned to the living room to pass them out. James and Tony were sitting on the floor by the coffee table, going through the bags. I offered a can to Alex, and he took it and nodded. I sat on the couch, and watched them.

"Have you heard the stories about this place?" James asked me. Without waiting for a response, he continued. "I'm not just talking about the boarding house," the ghost hunter continued. "This cottage is old, and it must've seen its fair share of deaths as well."

"I hadn't thought of that," I said, trying to not sound scared. It was one thing to think of ghosts by the sensible light of day, but thinking of such matters by night was yet another thing entirely. I most certainly did believe in ghosts, but in the time

I had been living in the cottage, I had not sensed so much as a single presence.

"Who ya gonna call?" the cockatoo screeched from behind me. I stood as Michael snickered beside me and James rolled his eyes. I put Max out the back door into the garden room. "It's night time, Max. Birds are supposed to be asleep at night."

"%&%$," was Max's reply, so I put him in his cage, put a cover over the cage, and returned to the living room.

"Sorry," I said to the group.

James frowned at me. "No problem, but we will need complete silence when we begin."

I nodded.

"Now, I wanted to let you know who we're trying to reach. I've done as much research as I can on this place, this cottage, the boarding house, and I think if we're going to reach anyone here, it's going to be Rebecca Settler."

I had never heard the name, but I knew James was itching to spill the beans, so I simply waited, and sure enough, he launched into an explanation.

"Rebecca Settler had an Irish father and an Australian mother. She had come to the boarding house in the late 1800's at the age of seventeen, after both of her parents died of a fever. She got a job as a maid for the wealthy people who then owned what is now the boarding house, and for a while she lived there. The gardener at the time was a man of twenty five years of age named Andrew. He and Rebecca fell in love, and married, and they moved to live here in this cottage. It was built just for them."

I yawned, and wished Mr Buttons had been present, but, as he pointed out, my cottage was simply not big enough for five people.

James was still talking. "Rebecca and Andrew were married for almost a year, when Abraham came to the boarding house. He was a friend of the owners, and he had been injured in some accident. I don't know, there's not too much written about it."

I listened with interest. I found myself taken in by the story, even though I couldn't be sure it was true.

James went on. "Rebecca was tasked with nursing Abraham back to health. They had spoken a lot, and as they came to know each other, they slowly fell in love. Now, Rebecca was torn between the two men, but she decided she wanted to be with Abraham. When he was well, and he was set to return to his own home, Rebecca came to pack her things up, she and Andrew got into a bad argument, and Rebecca ended up dead."

There was silence in the room. I had to admit it was a good story, and if James had made it up, I was impressed.

When James spoke again his voice was soft, haunting. "So, if someone is in this cottage, it's going to be Rebecca. I'd like to try to speak with her. She's stuck here," he added.

"Maybe she has unfinished business," Michael said, and Ken and Alex nodded.

"I've never seen her," I said.

"You can't always see ghosts," James said, his tone condescending. "Have you felt her?"

"No," I said truthfully. I was becoming increasingly annoyed with James. It was now obvious to me that he was lying, and I didn't appreciate it. If he believed in spirits, that was certainly fine with me—after all, I did, too. If James wanted to find proof of ghosts—well, he was welcome to do whatever he wanted. But to come here, and to tell me a story I suspected was completely fabricated, was really rubbing me the wrong way. I'd had enough; I stood up. I intended to say something rude, but was sidetracked by James taking up a theatrical pose in the centre of my living room, with Alex training a large camera on him.

"This is going to be a difficult investigation," he said, in a voice deeper than usual. "At this location we have two buildings, a boarding house and a cottage, and the resident spirits travel freely between them."

And then it was over. He stopped speaking, and Alex put down the large camera, and set up a smaller camera on a tripod. "Is it okay if we set up a camera, some REM pods and an EMF meter in your bedroom?" James asked.

"Sure," I said. I figured I might as well put up with it. After all, if one of these guys was the murderer, then I might get some clues after an all-night vigil with them in the close confines of my cottage.

"I need everyone to be silent, please," James said. "I'm going to speak into this recorder, and then leave it in Sibyl's bedroom for the night. Tomorrow, we'll listen to it and see anyone has responded to me." He motioned for us to be quiet, and for Alex to film him. "We've come a long way to talk to you," he said into the recorder. "Is anyone in here, in this cottage? Are you here, Rebecca? Are you here, Andrew? Please give us a sign that you're here."

He walked into my bedroom, with Alex following him, still filming.

The two returned moments later. "Now, that's set up," James said.

"Did you get any readings from the vigil at the boarding house?" I asked.

All four men nodded enthusiastically. "When we played back the audio, we heard all sorts of phenomena," Ken said. "Voices, a violin playing, a scream, and there was a threatening spirit who kept telling us to leave. Plus, we had a camera in James's room, and a small table in there rocked from side to side."

I tried to recall all the ghost hunting shows I had seen on TV—*Haunting Australia*, *Ghost Hunters*, *TAPS*, reruns of *Most Haunted*. "Do other ghost hunting shows get so much data?" I asked. "I mean, that sounds like a lot of stuff—more than I can remember seeing on TV."

"Oh, that's why the network wanted me to sign the deal," James gushed. "We have better equipment. I've tweaked all the equipment and we get much better results than anyone else." He smiled broadly, and I couldn't help but notice that Alex, Michael, and Ken stared at him with admiration plainly stamped all over their faces.

"We'll have to do it differently, as your cottage is so small," James said to me. "We'll all stay in this room with the cameras on and the voice recorders going. First of all, we have to walk around the room to make sure our readings won't be influenced by anything electrical."

I sat on the old, antique French chair and watched the four of them walk around with various forms of equipment. I was already having trouble staying awake, and the night was yet young. I suppressed a yawn, and wondered what James would say if I asked him if I could go to bed. I shook myself and reminded myself that I was here to catch a murderer. Cressida had very nearly fallen victim. Sure, Blake was back in town, but the bungling detectives were no doubt doing everything they could to shut the case down.

I looked around at the four men, James, Ken, Michael, and Alex. The fifth suspect was Dorothy. It was likely that one of the five was the murderer, so there were four out of five chances that the murderer was in my living room right now, and I was looking right at him. Of the four men, there was just something about James. Since meeting him, I had disliked him, then liked him, then tolerated him, and so on, back and forth. Something about him tonight, watching him with his lies, had made me uneasy. You either liked someone, or you didn't. I sat for a few more minutes, and then I fell asleep.

CHAPTER 18

*I* yawned widely as I rinsed the wriggling and squirming beagle puppy. It was an unusually busy day, with lots of last minute call ins. While I was grateful for the extra income, the timing was appalling—I was growing more tired by the minute.

I had known that giving into a ghost vigil would impact my work day. Life was chaotic enough without being part of some sort of supernatural reality television show, but I had hoped to gain some clue as to the identity of the murderer.

I wasn't sure what to make of the previous night. I was, however, sure of one thing—it would be weeks before I stopped jumping at drafts and shadows. Having the four of them jumping and making a big deal out of every noise for the entire night would no doubt have my imagination working overtime for some time to come.

I had to wonder if they really believed in their work. It was hard to believe when I had seen with my own eyes James's attempts to sensationalise their work with gasps and whispers to the camera. A greater problem was James's desire to capitalise on Sue's death. Even if James sincerely believed he could track signs of ghosts and such, it seemed cruel to hope his friend was now a spirit haunting the place. This surely was an intimate matter—not something to be shared on television.

Then again, to be fair, perhaps James's passion for his work had momentarily overridden his sense of decency. I remembered seeing a Dr. Phil episode on the strange and socially inappropriate things people did when dealing with grief. As long as it wasn't hurting anyone, there didn't seem to be a reason to make a scene of it.

I shook myself from my thoughts. I had to finish grooming all the dogs, drag myself home, and make dinner. I could only hope nothing came up before I got a quick shower and crawled into bed. I could barely stay awake now.

"Well Koda, you should be good to go," I said

to the impatient pup as I took him out of the tub and rubbed him down with a soft towel. He was so excited to be done with his bath that he spun in a tight circle with an excited whimper. I laughed as I dried him with the dryer.

"How are things going in here?" Koda's owner, Susan, asked as she made her way in with a tray bearing two coffee cups and several cup cakes.

"We're just finishing up." I smiled at the woman as I picked up a grooming brush, testing the fur to make sure Koda was dry before brushing him. Susan was a new client, having hired me only recently, within days after getting Koda for her children.

Susan set down the tray on a nearby table. "Are you feeling any better? You looked exhausted when you got here."

"Oh yes. It was just a long day today," I said, bending down to put Koda on a clean cushion in a crate. As I handed him a treat, I bemoaned the fact that I thought I had hidden my tiredness rather well, but obviously I hadn't. I needed to work on it before I went to my last two stops of the day.

"It seems like it." Susan handed me a mug of coffee and a cupcake.

"Thanks, Susan. I can't tell you how much I appreciate it."

"I imagine you've had your hands full," Susan said. "You live on the same property as that boarding house, correct? The one those ghost hunters are staying at?"

I could not help but detect a hint of something—concern or disapproval—in Susan's voice.

"That's right," I said, hoping Susan would say more.

Susan frowned. "I hope they're better behaved there than they are in town."

"What happened? What did they do in town?"

Susan shrugged. "I shouldn't have said anything. It's not anything really bad. I was just in town getting my prescriptions, and I saw one of them at odds with Dorothy. She and the boy were all but screaming at each other right in the middle of the street."

"Oh my." I was at a loss for words. I knew Dorothy had a bad temper, but why would she yell at one of the ghost hunters in the middle of town? "What happened exactly?" I asked. "Which one of the ghost hunters was it?"

"I'm not sure, to be honest. I was too far away to hear what they were arguing about. It was the man with the long black hair, if that helps any. The others hung back while he and Dorothy were having words with one another."

James. Why would James argue with Dorothy? "Do you know which one started it?" I asked.

Susan shook her head, "Sorry, I don't know. It did go on for some time, though. It gave all the locals something to watch." She laughed.

My mind whirled as I tried to think of a plausible reason those two would have to make a scene out in public. It wasn't as if they didn't run into each other often enough at the boarding house. They'd had plenty of opportunity to vent their frustrations in private. I would have thought Dorothy and James would have been professional enough to not take it to the streets.

"Maybe they said something about her cooking that didn't sit too well with her," I said. "Dorothy is quite touchy about her food."

"It didn't seem like that." Susan clucked her tongue. "It looked a lot more personal. They acted like they'd known each other for years. Something about it made me think it was something they'd fought about before. The others in his little group didn't even seem surprised they were fighting."

"Thanks for letting me know, Susan. And thanks for the coffee. I'll put it to good use."

Susan gave me a look of concern. "It's the least I can do. You'll make my life so much easier, making home visits."

My next two clients went smoothly. They were just shampoos, no clipping involved. I parked the van and bought a large take-out latté, which I consumed as quickly as I could. With my caffeine levels suitably elevated, I headed for the local library, which had free WiFi and three computers for public use, where I would be away from the ghost hunters and prying eyes.

I had rarely been in the library, which was new but quite small, as would be expected in a town with a population of around three thousand residents. There appeared to be no librarian in charge, although there was a man arranging tourist brochures near the entrance.

"Hello, where are you from?" he asked.

"Little Tatterford," I said, and the man's face fell with obvious disappointment.

"I'm just here to use the computers," I added.

He pointed to the back of the hall.

"Is there a charge for the computers?"

He looked at me as if I had grown three heads.

"Charge? No, it's funded by the Community Centre. We all need to support the Community Centre—they do several free services for the community. There's a Zumba class every night in the Community Hall, and Susan Palmer takes Boot Camp once a week. You run up the mountain carrying sandbags or tires." He handed me a stack of brochures.

"Sounds great," I spluttered, backing away after taking the brochures. "Some other time, perhaps. I just need to use the computers."

I hurried down to the back of the library, relieved that the man wasn't following me. The free Wifi was painfully slow, and the connection kept dropping out. I did manage to find an old photo of Dorothy, which I printed, and all it cost me was a coin donation and another conversation about fitness classes with the man.

CHAPTER 19

I sat on my couch next to Mr Buttons. He had a saucer and a cup of tea resting on his knee, and I had my laptop on my knees. It was mid morning, and I yawned and rubbed my eyes.

"So what are you doing exactly?" Mr Buttons asked me.

"I uploaded the old picture I found of Dorothy yesterday into my computer. I'm going to do an image search and see if anything comes up," I said.

"Right, that's what I thought," Mr Buttons said with a grin.

I pulled up the picture up of the email I had sent myself after scanning the photo down at the library. The photo was of the cook, although it was decades old. The picture was in black and white, and looked for all the world like a clipping from a newspaper. I was fairly confident I would be able to find it online.

I clicked on the picture and copied it the search engine. When I released it, a small circle appeared on the screen, spinning around as it searched. Jackpot. There was one link: *Local Woman Wins Bake Off*. The link took me to a site called *Newspaper Uploads*. I clicked on the link and waited.

It appeared as though the website simply took old newspapers and scanned them. There were hundreds of newspapers from across Australia, including the *Benalla Ensign*, which is where the picture of a young Dorothy was from.

"That's it!" Mr Buttons said, leaning over and taking a sip of his tea. I angled the screen so he could see better. Indeed, there was the black and white photo of Dorothy, accompanied by the article. The article said that the young Dorothy had won a national bake off, and this was the write-up in her hometown paper. The interesting thing, however, was that Dorothy's name wasn't Dorothy.

"They're calling her Samantha Ridley," Mr Buttons said, reaching out to tap the end of one of his long index fingers on the screen.

I murmured my agreement and leant closer to

the screen. The picture certainly looked like Dorothy.

I googled *Samantha Ridley*. Pages of links came up, and I went the tedious procedure of scrolling through them all.

"Why did she change her name?" Mr Buttons asked.

"This is why," I said. I had discovered Dorothy's blog. I was shocked that Dorothy even had a blog—who knew the woman even knew how to turn on a computer? I jabbed my finger at the screen. "Look, there's an old blog post: Samantha Dorothy Hicks—why I changed my name."

Mr Buttons rubbed his hands together. "Quick, see what it says."

It was a blog that Dorothy had written just three years ago. The blog said that she had changed her name as her husband had run off with another woman. Dorothy had then taken her middle name, and gone back to her maiden name. The rest of the lengthy post was about the ways in which her husband would burn in hell eternally.

Mr Buttons and I looked at each other. "Crikey," I said. "There's a lot of anger there."

Mr Buttons went to my kitchen to make another pot of tea, and I looked through more posts.

Most of the posts were about cooking, various recipes she liked, various cook jobs she'd had and lost. She seemed to lose a lot of jobs. I wasn't surprised, given the woman's temper. The interesting posts had less to do with cooking or food, and more to do with Dorothy's family. There were several posts about her nephew and the falling out he was having with his parents. He had finished his pharmacy degree, but he wasn't going to pursue a career as a pharmacist. A woman was pushing him into something else, but Dorothy did not mention what the something else was.

Mr Buttons and I read in silence, the older man leaning nearer after setting his tea on the coffee table before him. I was about to take a break and get something to eat, when I scrolled down to the next blog post, and my mouth fell open in shock.

This post had a picture. It was Dorothy, looking much more like her present self, and her nephew beside her. It was James.

I looked at Mr Buttons, and his face was one of shock as well. I couldn't believe it. I would never have guessed that they were related.

"You're kidding me," Mr Buttons said. "Why didn't they say anything?"

"I don't know," I said. "It looks like they had a

falling out at the same time that James and his parents did.

"Over a girl?"

I nodded. "It looks that way."

"I wonder what she wanted him to do?" he asked.

I had been wondering the same thing.

Mr Buttons tapped his chin. "The whole ghost business, perhaps? James is totally consumed by it now."

I leant forward and typed on the keyboard. I searched for James, and in no time, found his personal Facebook page. It appeared he had not used it in some time. I clicked on *Photos*, and the first photos to appear were those of Sue.

Mr Buttons and I turned to each other, but before we could speak, there was a knock on the door. I stood up, handed the laptop to Mr Buttons, and went to the door. Cressida stood on the porch, wearing a bright red sarong, and plenty of makeup on her face.

"I have information on James," she said, and threw her arms skywards in a dramatic gesture.

I had forgotten that Max was perched on the back of a chair. He had been uncharacteristically quiet. Now, however, Cressida's sudden appearance spurred him into action, or rather, speech. "You failed your IQ test!" he squawked.

I hurried over to him, but he flew away. I opened the back door, hoping he would fly straight out, but he landed, and slowly waddled towards the door. As he walked, he squawked something that sounded like, "Did you have a bad hair day, or do always look like that?"

I shut the door on him and turned back to Cressida. "What did you find out about James?" I asked.

"He has a pharmacy degree."

Mr Buttons and I exchanged glances. "Yes, we ourselves just found that," Mr Buttons said from the couch. Cressida moved to sit next to him, leaving the last cushion for me.

Mr Buttons reached over Cressida to hand the laptop back to me. "And listen to this," I said, turning the laptop a bit on my legs so Cressida could see the screen. I scrolled back through Dorothy's blog as I filled in Cressida on what they had found out. When I got to the part about Dorothy and James being related, Cressida gasped loudly and threw her hands to her mouth.

"You're kidding me," she said.

I shook my head. "It's for real. And get this,

James's girlfriend, the one who caused all of these problems, and made James' parents as well as Dorothy mad at him? That was Sue."

"No way," Cressida said, rearing back with her hand and slapping me on my arm.

"Ouch!" I rubbed my arm with my fingertips.

"So it's James," Cressida said. "He has pharmacy degree so would surely know about nicotine. Or it's Dorothy, or Samantha, whatever she's called."

"I'm afraid I have to agree with you," Mr Buttons said. "I believe we can safely discount Alex, Michael, and Ken. That leaves either James or Dorothy, or perhaps both of them, working together."

"I can understand that they had motive for Sue's murder," Cressida said slowly. "But what about me—what could they possibly have against me? I pay Dorothy well, and I've never once complained about her cooking."

I rubbed my temples in an attempt to alleviate the headache that was rapidly forming. "You know, Cressida, they likely didn't intend to murder you. You used the same bottle of hair dye that Sue had used. Plus, you weren't in your own bathroom. The murderer or murderers probably had no idea you were going to use it."

Cressida nodded. "That makes sense. It was an unopened bottle—and I only decided to use it on the spur of the moment. I looked in the mirror and saw I had a horrible amount of regrowth, and Sue and I had similar hair colouring. The package was sitting there."

"So what do we do now?" I asked. "Apart from giving all his information to Blake, of course."

No one spoke. "We need more," Mr Buttons said after a few moments.

"It's Dorothy," Cressida said, nodding her head. "I know it. I just know it. Why else would she change her name?"

"We know why she changed her name," I pointed out. "It says so on the blog."

"I just feel it in my bones," Cressida said. "I think this could be the first time that Lord Farringdon has it wrong. He insists it's not her, but cats don't know everything."

Mr Buttons and I exchanged glances, and Cressida saw us.

"You people are no help," Cressida said. "It looks like I'm going to have to solve this one on my own, like usual."

The three of us laughed.

I realised I felt happy. It was strange, to feel so happy in this situation. Here we were, once again trying to solve a horrible crime—a murder no less. Cressida herself had almost been killed this time. Yet I was happy, sitting with my two friends, two friends I never thought I would have, and as we talked about suspects and dug dirt up on people, I felt good. There was a time, just after my divorce, when I didn't think I would ever feel good. I had been proven wrong. It had just taken a little murder and mayhem.

Cressida's words brought me from my daydream. "Why don't we just confront her?" she asked. "Let's just tell her what we found out."

I shook my head, but Mr Buttons nodded. "What do we have to lose?" he asked, and then he looked directly at me. "Right?"

"I don't know. What if she escapes? Or worse still, pulls out a long knife?"

"She'd only do that if she was the killer," Cressida said.

"But isn't that the whole point of confronting her?" I asked. "Confronting on the basis that we suspect that she's the killer?"

"We need to let her know that we know, without

letting her know that we know, you know?" Cressida said.

I sat there, rubbing vigorously at my temples and trying to understand what Cressida just said. "Okay, I'll speak to her," I said. I stood up. "Let's go back to the boarding house."

When we arrived at the boarding house, Cressida and Mr Buttons went to make tea in the kitchen, and I went to Dorothy's room.

I suppressed a shudder, and knocked on her door.

"Who is it?" was the gruff reply.

"It's just me, Sibyl," I said my voice shaking.

"Come in!"

I walked through the door, taking deep breaths to calm myself. The cook was sitting on her bed, with a book in front of her.

"Can I speak with you?" I asked.

"Isn't that what you're doing?" she snapped.

*Oh great.* I figured that I might as well just blurt it all out. "James was talking, and, err, he called you his aunt."

Dorothy frowned deeply, and looked away from me. "That idiot," she said finally. "I knew he would do something like this."

"Why didn't you two tell anyone?" I asked.

Dorothy looked back at me. "Well, it's no one's business, is it? James is my nephew, but his parents have disowned him and so have I. It was a shock to see him again, and I didn't feel the need to tell anyone."

I took courage in the fact that Dorothy had not pulled out a long knife from under her pillow. I stayed close to the door, in case I had to beat a hasty retreat. "But when Sue died, and then Cressida was poisoned too, didn't you think it was relevant?"

Dorothy glared at me. "Why? I didn't have anything to do with Sue or Ms Upthorpe. Small towns are full of gossip. I told James to stay quiet about us being related."

"Why?" I asked.

Dorothy didn't answer right away. She kept her eyes averted, and then she took a deep breath and spoke. "Sue was his girlfriend—she was the reason that James' parents disowned him. When she died, I didn't want anyone to know I was his aunt, and that I hadn't cared for her much. James was a good kid, you know? He had so much promise, more promise than my dunce of a son ever showed. But then that girl came along, and she filled his head with ghosts this, and ghosts that, and all of this other devilish nonsense. He threw away his promising career."

I was surprised how easily Dorothy was confessing, yet the fact remained that she wasn't trying to hide anything, which made me wonder whether she was the killer, after all.

"Is there anything else you want to tell me?" I asked.

Dorothy looked at me with narrowed eyes, her brows dipping low on her forehead. Then she sighed, and got out of bed. "I have to go start cooking," she said.

As she headed towards me, I said, "Okay, thanks," and hurried out the door first, just in case she was the killer, after all.

I reached the dining room in double quick time, and found Cressida and Mr Buttons in the dining room, sipping tea. I sat next to Mr Buttons, who poured tea into a delicate, bone china cup and set it in front of me. I dropped some sugar into it and stirred it with a small spoon, leaving Cressida and Mr Buttons on the edge of their seats.

"She admitted she was James's aunt," I whispered, aware that the kitchen wasn't too far from the dining room. I could hear Dorothy in there; water was running, pots and pans were banging.

Cressida wrung her hands. "If she's the killer, if

she poisoned me, we need to know. I don't feel safe; I don't want her here."

"I don't think she's the killer, Cressida," I said.

"What makes you say that?" she asked.

"I don't know," I said truthfully. "It's just a hunch."

CHAPTER 20

*A* sense of anticipation had descended upon the boarding house. There was something exciting about the fact that a television content executive was coming to the boarding house, even if no one knew exactly what a television content executive did.

I had heard about it that morning from Cressida. Her phone had started ringing at five in the morning, and I grabbed it from my nightstand and answered it. I had been groggy, and sleepy, and not a little irritated that someone would call me so early.

"What are you doing for lunch?" Cressida asked as soon as I had said *hello*.

"It's five in the morning," I had said.

"I know, I know. And the answer to the question I asked you is that you're coming down here for lunch, because a Hollywood hot shot is coming to speak with James and his team."

"What?" I asked, waking up. I had sat up in my bed, leaning back against the headboard.

"He's a network content executive. That's what I heard James saying, anyway."

I narrowed my eyes. "You heard him saying that at five in the morning?"

"No, I heard him saying that at four in the morning. I just happened to be near his room, and he was talking on the phone with someone."

"Interesting," I said.

"Interesting? A Hollywood type is coming here, and he'll be here at lunch time, so you better get down here."

"Okay, I will," I had said.

"Good. See you at eleven. You can help me make sandwiches."

"What about Dorothy?"

"I can't trust her to make lunch, in case she poisons us all. I've given her the day off."

I laughed and hung up. I set my phone back on the table and went back to sleep.

I was at the boarding house at eleven on the

dot. I walked up the front steps and pushed the door open. No one was in the hall, so I continued on to the kitchen, where I found Cressida making a big bowl of potato salad.

"I didn't want to get too fancy," Cressida said by way of greeting. "I figured someone from television has enough fancy food."

"I'm sure he does."

"Full disclosure—I'm missing one of my nails," Cressida said as she held her right hand out to me so I could see that one of the garish pink acrylic nails had come off her index finger. "I think it's in here, so keep an eye out, all right?"

I grimaced and nodded.

"And can you start making sandwiches? Everything is there."

There wasn't a lot of time to speak with all the work to be done, so the two of us hunkered down and got lunch ready. By noon there was a nice spread on the dining room table: various sandwiches, the potato salad, a macaroni salad, a large pitcher of ice tea, another of lemonade, along with a few bags of potato chips, and a platter of cupcakes for dessert. For an added plus, the fake nail had been found, indeed in the potato salad.

Cressida opened the door from the dining room

to the main hall to find it filled with people. Mr Buttons was there, as was James, Ken, Michael, and Alex. There was a good looking man of about fifty years of age wearing an expensive suit. His hair was black and slicked back, and he wore sunglasses which he pulled off and slid into his breast pocket before shaking Cressida's hand.

"My name is Victor Fredricks, and I think you all might have known I was coming."

This drew a laugh from the ghost hunters. I would have laughed too, if I had been expecting a rich contract.

"We have lunch ready for everyone," Cressida said.

"Thank you," Victor said, before turning to James. "Let's eat, and then you and I can discuss what I came here to discuss."

"Sounds great, Mr Fredericks," James said. James' face was flushed with excitement.

"Please, call me Victor."

"Okay, Victor."

And with that we all went into the dining room and ate lunch. I sat a few seats down from Victor, who was enthralling us all with stories of Hollywood, and personal details about celebrities he knew. I hung on every word. It was simply cool. I didn't know a better word to describe it.

When lunch was finally over, two and a half hours later, Victor turned to Cressida.

"Would you please excuse us? James and I have a few things we need to go over."

"Of course," Cressida said with a smile.

Everyone filed out of the dining room, and Cressida and I cleared the table.

I was stacking the dishwasher when Cressida said, "I'll go and see if I can hear anything."

I just nodded and kept shoving as much as I could in the dishwasher.

I had just dumped the dishes that didn't fit into the dishwasher into the sink and was filling it with hot sudsy water, when Cressida returned. "What are they talking about?"

"I don't know," she said. "I've heard the words *contract*, *prime time*, and that's about all I can make out. Oh, and I'm sure I heard the words *million dollars*."

My mouth fell open. "A million dollars?"

Cressida nodded.

"So that was why he killed Sue," a voice said, and I turned to see Dorothy standing by the sink.

"You think James killed Sue?" Cressida asked. "Why didn't you say anything?"

"I didn't want him to kill me," Dorothy said.

"Why do you think your James killed Sue?" I asked, keeping an eye on the knife drawer, just in case.

Dorothy took a step closer to me. "I heard them arguing, the night before Sue died."

"About what?" I asked as I moved further away from Dorothy.

"Sue was mad at James. She said he was faking everything, and she didn't want to be a part of it. Sue had said she wouldn't let him do that. She said she would tell everyone. And the next day she was dead."

At that moment, the door swung open, and Victor walked into the room.

"I didn't mean to scare you, although when you're in a house this haunted, I'm not surprised you're all on edge!" the man said with a smile. His teeth were so white they were almost blinding. I supposed that everyone in Hollywood had teeth like that. "I just want to thank you for a lovely lunch, and it was great to meet you all, and I have a plane to catch."

"You're all done?" Cressida asked. "That was fast."

"Well you know what they say in Hollywood," Victor said. "Hurry up and wait." He winked and then left.

"Well, we had better call Blake," Cressida said, when the door shut. "And we had better call him fast."

CHAPTER 21

Mr Buttons kept an eye on the window while I searched James' bedroom, looking for evidence to indicate that James was faking the ghostly phenomena.

"Hurry, Sibyl! James will probably be heading back soon."

"I know, but we have to find something first." I rummaged through suitcases and duffel bags, when my eyes fell upon some furniture in the corner. I walked over and lifted up a round, wooden table. It looked heavy and old, but I was able to flip it right-side up with one hand. "Mr Buttons, come here! I think I've found something."

He walked over and looked at the table without even a hint of optimism on his face. "A table?"

"Not just a table. Look at this." I handed the table to Mr Buttons and tilted it so he could see a metallic device that was fastened to the bottom of the table. "I think it's for a signal or something. Look, there's even a remote."

Mr Buttons reached over and slid the remote from its holster. He pressed a few buttons on the tiny remote, and the table shook.

"Wow, so this is how he did it," I said. "One press of a button and it looks like a ghost is randomly shaking the table."

Mr Buttons pointed to a strange-looking contraption poking from a black, duffel bag. "See what that is."

I leant over, and seized the device. It was square in shape, with large antennae, several LED lights decorating the top, and a gauge with a floating needle resting in the centre. I pressed one of the buttons, and a ghostly voice emanated from the other side of the room.

I jumped and clutched at my throat. "That scared me," I said, somewhat unnecessarily.

"He's set it up so that if you press that button, the ghostly voice comes out of that camera," Mr Buttons said. He crossed the room and fetched the camera. "Press the button again, Sibyl."

I did, and the ghostly voice said, "Leave!"

"That was the voice we heard the other night," I said.

Mr Buttons nodded. "Yes, and with the cameras being in the other rooms, no one would know the voices were actually coming from the cameras. Sibyl, we have enough. Let's take the camera and the EMF meter and get out of here."

I looked around the room which was in disarray. "No, we'd better cover our tracks first. Mr Buttons, could you hurry and call Blake, and tell him to get here fast, and I'll quickly put everything back, so that James won't know anyone's been through his things."

Mr Buttons nodded in agreement and headed towards the door. "All right, but make it fast! He could be back at any minute."

I set the table back down in its original location and tidied up as best I could. I heard the door open, and I swung around.

"What do you think you're doing up here?" James's tone was filled with fury.

"I'm sorry. I came up here to look for you, and the door was open. I just thought it would be cool to see some of your ghost hunting gadgets."

James turned around and locked the door behind him. "You do realise I'm not stupid, right?"

"Err, umm," I stammered.

"So you thought you'd come up here and look through my gear for what? To find a motive for Sue's murder? Did you find one?"

"A motive?" I parroted.

He looked at me in disgust. "I see you're standing right near my table, and I'm sure you've already found out that it's rigged to make it look like paranormal activity is affecting it. Also, I supposed you've discovered that the EMF detectors are rigged to go off whenever I want them to."

No, I hadn't known that. "So what if your show's a bit staged?" I said. "I watch a lot of TV. I'm sure it's all staged."

James walked towards me and I backed against the wall. "Sue was going to blow the whistle and come out with the truth. Sue and I dated on and off for a long time. We pretty much started this thing together. Sue objected when I faked stuff for the pilot. So, I told her we needed to part ways and that I'd make sure she was compensated for being in the pilot. That was not something she was willing to accept though. She told me she had emails, photographs, video, and everything else she needed to prove I was a fraud. She even threatened to go to the network with the information and demand she stay on the show."

"So she was going to use extortion as a way of staying in the TV series?" I said, hoping to keep him talking until help arrived. "Surely the network would have dealt with it themselves."

James let out a snort of derision. "No. They would have cancelled the entire thing. It was worth over a million bucks to me—did you hear that? A million bucks!"

"So you killed her?"

James shrugged. "I didn't have a choice. I injected nicotine into her hair dye—quite clever of me, I thought."

"Well, you nearly killed Cressida, too."

"I didn't mean for anyone else to get hurt. Well, until now." Without a warning, he lunged towards me and seized me by my arm. With his fingers digging painfully into my arm, he dragged me over to the open window.

I threw myself backwards, and I collapsed to the ground, pulling James down with me. James scrambled back to his feet, and grabbed me with both hands. "Don't make this any harder than it needs to be."

James dragged me to the window, and when I caught sight of the ground below, I struggled even harder. It was a long drop to the ground, with James's room being two stories up, and I knew I wouldn't survive the fall. I screamed, but James clamped his hand over my mouth. I smashed the window next to the opening to dry to draw attention to my plight, but all that did was cut my hand.

At that moment, the door flew open with a loud thud. As James looked up in surprise, I took the opportunity to knee him hard in the unmentionables. I ran forward, and staggered into Blake's arms. "He killed Sue," I said.

"I'll take care of him. Keep her safe and get her outside," Blake said to Mr Buttons, who was right behind him. He turned back towards the room and shut the door.

I crumpled into Mr Buttons' arms as we both fell against the wall and slid to a sitting position.

There were a few loud noises and banging sounds from within the room, and then Blake opened the door, pushing a handcuffed and sullen-faced James in front of him.

CHAPTER 22

*Learn How to Kill in Just Three Swift Techniques.* I sighed and dropped the brochure—that one might be a bit too much. *On Efficient and Tactical Threat Neutralisation.* That one was clearly out of my league. *How to Rip a Man in Half.* Hmm.

I leant back in my chair and threw my hands into the air in defeat. I'd been leafing through self-defence brochures all day but hadn't had any luck. It didn't seem like many people wanted—or were able—to teach martial arts in such a small town, and the few that did seemed, quite frankly, terrifying.

Given that James had attacked me, learning how to defend myself seemed like the natural next step. I knew it wasn't something that was likely to ever happen again (or in the first place, I supposed), but learning a martial art would be a good way to set myself at ease.

Then again, I considered that I was already quite at ease. Life was back to normal, and I'd finally found the chance to relax. I was halfway through my coffee when my thoughts were interrupted.

"Shut up, you &^%$$ idiot!" Max yelled, much to my surprise. Through quick thinking, I narrowly avoided spilling my coffee all over myself by nimbly spilling it all over the table. I sighed, setting the cup down and grabbing a cleaning cloth. Just as I finished cleaning it up, I was interrupted again, this time by a knock on the door. I threw the sponge in the sink and quickly finished rinsing my cup out before answering it.

As the door opened, the first thing I noticed was that someone was holding a bunch of flowers. The second thing I noticed was Blake. Finally, I noticed that he was wondering why I was still looking at the flowers and hadn't said anything.

"Uh, hello, Sibyl," he said, leaning down and giving me a little wave.

I felt my face turning red and quickly composed

myself. "Hello, Blake, sorry! I was just lost in thought." I smiled.

He chuckled and handed the flowers to me. "These are for you. I thought I should check up on you after everything that's happened."

I took the flowers, admiring them. I had no idea what kinds they were, but they were a vibrant myriad of colours and shapes. Some of the flowers were completely foreign to me, but it was a beautiful arrangement.

"Thanks so much!" I said. I hugged him on impulse and he hugged me back. We both lingered a little longer than was normal before releasing, and I felt my face turning red again. I looked up at him, as we were still holding each other. He looked back, his face inches from mine. I leant in, thinking that we might be about to kiss.

"#$^& off! You stink!" Max yelled furiously from inside. We released each other and both took a step back, embarrassed.

"Um, come in, come in," I said, ushering him through the door and looking at the floor. My face was red again, and Blake was the last person I wanted noticing.

"Do you have company?" he asked, looking for the source of the yell. "I didn't mean to intrude."

"No!" I exclaimed before composing myself. "That's Max, as usual. He still hasn't given up his bad language." I laughed nervously. "Would you like some coffee?" I started the machine and, hopefully, a new topic of conversation.

"Sure, thanks." He smiled and took a seat. "I can't talk about specifics just yet, but I wanted to let you know that you don't have to worry about James. That's all in the past." He smiled again.

I turned around from the coffee machine to face him. "I'd figured as much, but it's still good to hear," I said, turning back and finishing the first coffee. "The evidence against him wasn't exactly circumstantial." I handed Blake his drink and went back to making my own.

Blake laughed a little, nodding. "Not exactly, no. How are you holding up?" he asked, a look of genuine concern in his eyes. It wasn't until that moment that I realised it wasn't normal for police to follow up on this sort of thing personally, even in a small town like this.

"I'm fine, but I appreciate you asking." I poured my coffee and sat down opposite Blake. "It was scary, of course, but I know it's not something that can affect me again."

"Are you, uh, planning anything?" Blake picked

up one of the self-defence brochures: *How Enemies Become Dead.* He raised an eyebrow and looked at me with concern.

"Just leafing through a few of them, but I don't think they're for me, if I'm honest. I'm not at all a fan of violence, even if it's in self-defence." I drank my coffee slowly, trying to savour it. I was enjoying just sitting here with Blake, even if the air was a little heavy and I didn't know what to talk about.

"Do you think…" I was interrupted again by yet another knock on the door. "Oh, excuse me," I said, standing up. I opened the door to see Cressida and Mr Buttons, both smiling broadly and handing me a bouquet of flowers. For the briefest moment I worried that Cressida was going to try and kiss me.

"Hi, Sibyl!" Cressida said, still smiling broadly. "We thought we should check on you. How are you holding up?" Mr Buttons stood behind her, wearing a look of concern.

"I'm fine, thank you! And thanks for the flowers." I smiled back. "I'm just here with Blake," I said, hoping they would get the hint.

"Oh, I'd like to say thank you to him," Cressida said, completely oblivious and walking straight past me into the house. Mr Buttons gave me a quick hug and followed her inside.

I looked down at the flowers they had given me. I put them in a vase and added some water, setting it on a high side table where Sandy wouldn't knock it over. Blake, Cressida, and Mr Buttons were chatting in the next room and I went back to join them.

"Anyone for a drink?" I was asking in order to be polite, but was hoping they'd leave me alone with Blake for a moment. It seemed as though whenever I was with Blake it was either somewhere very public or somebody was trying to kill somebody else. This was one of the precious few times we were having a moment together, so I should have known from the outset that something would interrupt it.

Not that I minded too much. It was a little frustrating, but it was good to have my friends in one place now that there wasn't anything to worry about.

"Oh, yes, please!" Cressida said, much too excited.

"Yes, thank you, Sibyl," Mr Buttons said politely. "Would you like a hand?"

"That's fine, thanks. It won't take long." I smiled and exchanged glances with Blake, who apparently felt the same way that I did. It wasn't a bad thing to have them here, though, and Blake and I would always have time later.

"What exactly are you doing?" Blake asked. I spun around to see Mr Buttons on his knees, polishing Blake's shoes furiously.

"Just a spot of dirt," Mr Buttons explained nonchalantly. "Oh, it's a stubborn one, though." He continued scrubbing furiously. Blake sat patiently, unsure of how to react.

"Mr Buttons, please leave Blake alone. He's a police officer, so his shoes are going to get dirty from time to time. They'll get dirty again as soon as you leave, there's no point in cleaning them now." I noticed Mr Buttons wasn't really paying attention to me as I spoke, continuing to try and rub the dirt from Blake's shoes.

Eventually, he was satisfied. He sat back down at the table and smiled as though nothing had happened. Blake was wearing an expression somewhere between stunned and horrified. I brought the coffees back and sat them in front of the two newer guests.

"Thank you Sibyl," Cressida said, placing her glasses on the table and taking a sip. "Great as always!" she continued cheerily.

The four of us got to talking—about recent

events, events long past, and events yet to take place. The conversation was casual and easygoing, a happy contrast to recent goings on.

"Oh, no, Sandy!" I exclaimed, shooting out of my chair. Sandy had run into the room and grabbed Cressida's glasses from the table without so much as acknowledging us. She had then decided to run back outside and play with them in the yard. I started to give chase, but Cressida put her hand on my arm.

"I think they're long gone, Sibyl," she said forlornly. "I'm not sure I really want them back now anyway. Dog saliva doesn't do much for my vision." As Cressida said it, she pulled out an identical pair of glasses and put them on. All the time I'd known her, Cressida still found strange new ways to be weird. Not that I really minded.

"Oh!" she exclaimed suddenly. "I forgot to tell you all that I have a new artwork to show. I'll just go grab it."

"I have to leave," Blake said flatly before Cressida could so much as move. I glared at him as best I could, hoping he'd take the hint that I didn't want to be left alone.

"Actually, uh, never mind," he said, sitting back down, defeated.

"Sorry, Cressida, but I seem to have misplaced your painting before we visited," Mr Buttons said. "I just now remembered. Such a shame. I'm sorry."

Cressida looked a little disappointed, but I felt an immense sense of relief. Blake went so far as to sigh loudly. I wondered if it was possible to have Mr Buttons recommended for some kind of medal.

"Oh well," I said. "Next time, I suppose." I wondered how I could avoid ever having to see it, but resigned myself to the inevitability. We all chatted for a long time afterwards—at least two more hours, possibly more—before Blake received a phone call.

"I'm afraid I've been called into work," he said sadly. "I'll come over again some time soon."

"Yes, please do," Cressida said happily, apparently missing the point entirely.

"Just please wipe your shoes before you come in." Mr Buttons wore a stern look as he spoke, and it was entirely impossible to tell whether or not he was joking.

"I, uh, I will," Blake stammered. "Bye, everybody. Bye, Sibyl." He gave me another smile. I said my goodbyes and turned back to Cressida and Mr Buttons.

"I suppose we should be going, too. We'll come visit you later on," Cressida said.

"Please, do. You know you two are always welcome," I said earnestly. *Well on second thoughts, almost always*, I added silently.

Mr Buttons and Cressida walked out the door. I waved to them as they walked away and then went back to the coffee machine for another one. As they say—or rather, as *I* say—five coffees a day keep the doctor away.

I sat down and thought it was good to have friends like these, and finally, peace to share with them.

NEXT BOOK IN THIS SERIES

The Prawn Identity

*There's something fishy in Little Tatterford. Can Sibyl solve the murder and make a snapper comeback?*

There hasn't been a murder in weeks, so Sibyl and her eccentric friends, Cressida Upthorpe and Mr. Buttons, are able to scale back their anxiety. Honeymooners, a famous businessman and his wife, book in to start their married life in bliss. After a breakfast of prawns, a tragic accident befalls one of them and they end up battered. The authorities, herring rumors, want to shut down the boarding house for safety reasons.

The police believe the husband was the target but

are all at sea and unable to catch a break. The protesters rally against the husband's company, which is destroying the local wilderness land. Will he rise to the bait?

What with Blake's ex-girlfriend coming back to town, and a rival boarding house opening up nearby, can Sibyl keep a cool head, reel in the suspects, and save the boarding house from the authorities?

ABOUT MORGANA BEST

USA Today Bestselling author Morgana Best survived a childhood of deadly spiders and venomous snakes in the Australian outback. Morgana Best writes cozy mysteries and enjoys thinking of delightful new ways to murder her victims.

www.morganabest.com